SCOUSE

ALL YOU NE

SCOUSE GOTHIC

3

ALL YOU NEED IS... BLOOD?

IAN MCKINNEY

YOUCAXTON PUBLICATIONS

OXFORD & SHREWSBURY

Contents

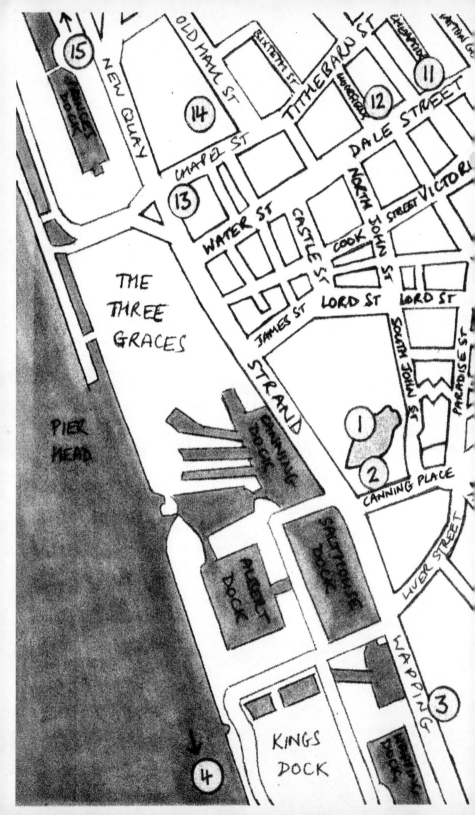

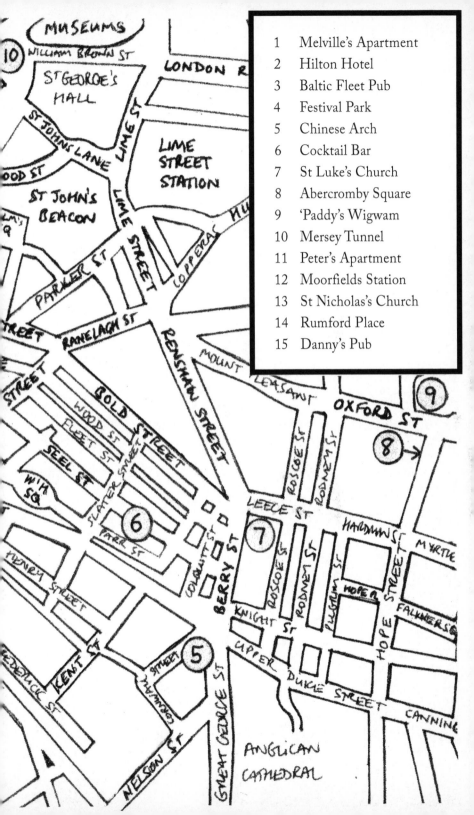

1   Melville's Apartment
2   Hilton Hotel
3   Baltic Fleet Pub
4   Festival Park
5   Chinese Arch
6   Cocktail Bar
7   St Luke's Church
8   Abercromby Square
9   'Paddy's Wigwam
10   Mersey Tunnel
11   Peter's Apartment
12   Moorfields Station
13   St Nicholas's Church
14   Rumford Place
15   Danny's Pub

The Strand

BEEP... BEEP... BEEP...

'Would you like a bag luv?' the cashier asked without enthusiasm.

'No thanks—I've got one here.' Lathom took a carrier bag from his left pocket. He liked to be prepared for any eventually—he had a 'Chow Mein' special in his right pocket just in case.

'That'll be £8.45—got a club card?'

Lathom shook his head and packed his bag, then handed her the money. He thought Sheryl had warned him about all the pros and cons of being a vampire but she appeared to have neglected to mention that he would feel permanently hungry.

It seemed to him that he'd done nothing but eat for the last two weeks, since he'd left hospital. He'd been on diets off and on for years, well, mainly off if he was being truthful. The Cambridge Diet, Weight-watcher's, Atkins and many others—he'd tried them all but none had worked. Now he realised, all people needed to do was get bitten by a vampire—perhaps he should market it: 'Lose pounds and gain immortality with the V-plan diet.'

The change in his appearance had been remarkable; he'd lost nearly three stones but had also gained muscle.

If it carried on at this rate he'd look like a bald Arnold Schwarzenegger by Christmas. He'd joined the gym in the base of the apartment block and also started jogging. But it wasn't all positive. The dreams and hallucinations had begun and, perhaps more depressingly, he could no longer get drunk. This last symptom was the most disturbing; he loved his whisky and the gentle oblivion of alcohol but now he was stone cold sober all the time. Lathom had begun to appreciate that eternity could be a very long time indeed.

He left the small supermarket and walked back down the Strand towards his apartment deep in thought. The last few weeks had seen a major changes in all aspects of his life. He was no longer a lonely alcoholic close to death; he was now an immortal vampire with a daughter and granddaughter. It had seemed an easy choice in the hospital: a slow and no doubt painful death alone, or eternity and a family. Now he was beginning to have his doubts.

The dreams and hallucinations were little different from the sort he had had previously with alcohol, but the desire for blood was something new. He'd seen a lot of blood in his past, but it had always been the unfortunate by-product of the job—not the reason for it.

Since that day in the hospital he'd only talked briefly to Sheryl about the reality of being a vampire and even then she'd made a joke of it. Consequently, he still felt out of his depth and unsure as to what to do next. He assumed that as he'd had several blood transfusions in the hospital that had somehow supressed his desire to kill, but when that returned—what did he have to do? Would he need a lot of blood? How often? How did you harvest it?

Lathom entered the block and nodded at Phil the concierge who was deep in conversation with a foreign resident. He took the lift to the 13th floor and was about to open the door to his apartment, 13F, when the fire alarm went off.

Suddenly the door of 13C opposite flew open and Sheryl ran out coughing. Lathom dropped his shopping and taking his 'Chow Mein' special from his coat pocket rushed inside her apartment. It was full of smoke. He quickly checked all the rooms and by the time he returned to the kitchen Sheryl was scraping a black piece of toast into the sink and his shopping was on the table.

'Hiya Bobby—fancy some toast? They say charcoal is good for the digestion.'

Lathom sat down and put his gun on the table. 'Thought it was something to do with Kelly.'

'Think we've seen the last of him, Bobby.'

'Really?'

'Well, for the time being anyway.' Sheryl put two pieces of toast on a plate in front of him. 'Butter's on the side—honey or marmite?'

'Honey,' Lathom wrinkled his nose, '– have you got any low fat spread?'

'No—and don't worry butter won't kill you,' she laughed. 'Afraid the honey is from Lidl—I suppose now you're on this health kick all your honey is from Waitrose and made by virgin bees?'

'Worker bees are all virgins.'

'Is that why they're always buzzing about—looking for boy bees?'

Lathom ignored her and began to eat his burned toast. 'Tea or coffee?' Sheryl asked.

'Whisk… Tea, no sugar.'

'You've really got it bad, Bobby—cut out the booze too?'

'Doesn't taste the same now—or have the same effects.'

'You'll get used to it. Don't bother trying drugs; they won't get you high either.'

'What does?'

'Sex can be fun—but for a real buzz you need blood.'

Lathom decided to seize the moment. 'What do you do?' he asked. It was a delicate subject.

'Well, you just drink it, Bobby. That's it. You don't need much—a cup full perhaps'

'How often?'

'Depends—everyone's different. Lee went years once—but he's odd. Longest I've gone is six months. You'll know when—it's like all addictions; you get a sort of itch.'

'How do you get it—the blood?'

'I use my penknife. I don't know about Lee—we never talk about things like that. You sort of find your own way I suppose. Becoming a vampire is usually an accident so it doesn't come with a *User's Manual*. We're only talking about it at all because I feel a bit responsible for you, Bobby.'

'You don't need to. It was my decision—I knew what I was getting myself into.'

'Did you, Bobby? I hope you won't regret it and blame me?'

'Course not. I'd never have got to know Michelle and Natasha without it.'

'How's that going?'

'It's early days—just getting to know each another. I'm meeting Michelle for lunch today.'

'That what's in the shopping bag?'

'No, that's just a mid-morning snack.'

'Still eating for three or four are you? It'll pass, it's just your body changing itself. It'll soon level off. You'll know when you've completely changed.'

'How?'

'You'll be able to sense the rest of us.'

'What do you mean *sense*?'

'You'll know if one of us in near. It's sort of like when you feel the hairs on the back of your neck rise at the threat of danger.'

'Why danger?'

'Usually we don't get along too well—it's a territorial thing I suppose, a bit like tom cats or tigers; there's no love lost between us.'

'What about you and Lee?'

'We just sort of hit it off straight away. Usually it's more like Lee and Kelly. So be warned—when you get the urge, make sure they're dead, OK?'

Lathom nodded. His mouth was full of toast which he swallowed, washing it down with a mouthful of tea.

'What about having kids?' he asked.

'As a light snack?'

'Vampire kids—can you and Lee have kids of your own?'

'No—immortality is the best form of contraception. Young vampires have always been young; old vampires have always been old. In fact, keep away from the adolescent ones, Bobby; they're unpredictable and dead nasty.'

'Are there many of *us* around?'

'Not really sure to be honest. As I said, we keep out of one another's way and no one wants to draw attention to themselves. Sometimes you only become aware that there must be one of us in the area by the report of a missing person or of a murder.'

'Have you met many besides Lee and Kelly?'

'A few—here, let me get you some more tea and toast.'

Sheryl seemed keen to change the subject so he decided not to pry into her past. She put more bread in the toaster and switched on the kettle.

'I've been meaning to ask, Bobby—why did the police close the case? An abduction, an attempted robbery and two gunshot victims in the city centre—and it's all been swept under the carpet. No one charged, even that scally of Kelly's gets let off—why?'

'They were told to back off.'

'By who?'

'Friends of mine—well, "ex-employers" would be more accurate.'

'What happened?'

'That snotty DI came to see me in hospital but I wouldn't talk. Luckily our friend Peter did what I asked him to do, and hid my gun and the handcuffs, so they didn't have much to go on. And Kelly's thug knew it would be unwise to talk—I'm sure he's more frightened of Kelly than of a few months inside.'

'And they left it at that?'

'Not quite—he tried threatening me, but I know how it works. I've done his job in the past, a bit of carrot and stick. It was quite amusing until I got bored with it.'

'What did you do then, Bobby?'

'I said, "My name is Robert George Lathom," then I quoted the *Official Secrets Act*. Told him who to phone and to tell them it was to do with "Operation Unicorn".'

'Was that it?'

'I also told him to fuck off and let me get some rest.'

Sheryl laughed. 'What happened then?'

'I assume he phoned them and they told him to forget it had ever happened.'

'What was Operation Unicorn?' Sheryl was always curious.

'Something from a long time ago that my old employers are keen to keep dead and buried.'

'So you do know where they buried the bodies,' Sheryl laughed. 'It wasn't a joke after all?'

'Any chance of some more toast?' It was Lathom's turn to change the subject.

Sheryl smiled, she knew he'd tell her one day.

'So you don't feel sick?' she asked as he took another bite of toast.

'When I wake up I do—every morning,' said Lathom between mouthfuls, '-but it soon passes and then I feel hungry again.'

'That'll pass, same as the dreams and hallucinations.'

'I know you warned me—but they're weird.'

'Yeah, I know—but don't worry, Bobby, it'll stop soon. Then you'll stop eating me out of house and home.' Sheryl cleared away the plates and Lathom realised that he'd eaten all her breakfast too.

'Sorry.' He was embarrassed.

'No worries. It's good to see you're on the mend.'

'Where's Lee?'

'On one of his walks again.' Sheryl raised her eyes to the ceiling.

'Where does he go?'

'Don't know, Bobby—I've asked God but he won't let on.'

'Sorry?' Lathom was confused. Had she just mentioned God? Perhaps he was hallucinating again because she ignored his question and continued to put the plates in the dishwasher. He realised that he'd outstayed his welcome; picked up his shopping bag, thanked her for the snack and slipped away.

That afternoon he was sitting in the *Baltic Fleet* waiting for his recently-discovered daughter, Michelle. They'd met a few times since he'd left hospital. Sheryl had got them together after she'd recognised her sister Jean in Lathom's old photo album and put two and two together from something Jean had told her in the nursing home.

Lathom had been shocked to realise that he had a daughter and a granddaughter that he never knew existed. When Jean had left all those years ago neither of them had had an inkling that she was carrying their child; she'd gone back to her old boyfriend Davy unaware that she was pregnant and it wasn't until Michelle was born with Lathom's bright red hair that it became obvious who her father was. The relationship with Davy hadn't been strong enough to survive that revelation but she'd had no desire to return to the angry, alcoholic who Lathom had turned into after Billy Flanagan's murder. Jean had moved back to live near her family in Liverpool while Lathom had been posted to Belfast.

He was sitting at the table in the bay window and looking down the Strand watching for Michelle when he heard a noise behind him. Turning, he saw a man sitting at the table next to him, naked and covered in blood.

'You should have come with me Bobby—then I'd still be alive.'

'I know you're a hallucination, Billy,' said Lathom calmly. 'Can you leave me to have my lunch in peace?'

The man disappeared and Lathom sipped his pint. He'd be glad when these hallucinations finished. He was used to dealing with guilt but being reprimanded by the dead was something new. Suddenly Michelle appeared through the crowd clutching her handbag and a carrier bag and he stood up and awkwardly kissed her on the cheek.

'Can I get you a drink? What would you like?'

'Dry white wine thanks, Bob—sorry—Dad?'

Lathom smiled. 'Bob will do—don't think I've earned Dad yet.'

There was an awkward silence as they sipped their drinks then both started talking at the same time, stopped at the same time—and laughed.

'I wish your mum was here too,' he said.

'Yeah, so do I,' Michelle looked slightly tearful, 'She used to talk about yer, but I didn't know you wer' me dad.'

'Did she—really?'

'She said she had a boyfriend who was a bizzie.'

'Special Branch,' Lathom muttered.

'Used to make her laugh by wigglin''is ears.'

Lathom wiggled his ears and they both laughed.

'She say anything else?'

'She said he wer a good lad, but too fond of a bevvie.'

Lathom's smile faded. 'Your mum was always a good judge of character.'

'I've brought you summin'– Bob.' She handed him the carrier bag she had been carrying. He pulled out a hand-knitted jumper and held it up. It had a snowman on the front.

'It's lovely—thanks…' He was touched that she'd knitted it for him but puzzled by the snowman.

'It wer the only pattern I 'ad,' she explained. 'Is it a bit big?'

He took off his coat and tried it on; it was about two sizes too large.

'That's funny—I thought you wer a lot fatter—bigger boned?' She tugged at the loose front.

'I'm dieting. Probably put it all back on for Christmas.' He leaned over and kissed her on the cheek.

'How's Natasha doing now?' he asked.

'A bit better, but what with the kidnapping and then me mam's funeral she hasn't been 'erself. The doctor says she's got post-traumatic whatsit; he's sent 'er for counselling.'

'Is she still seeing things?'

'Only me mam, I think. The doc sez yer sometime do that when yer grieving but me and Pete are still worried about 'er. She norra self; gone all moody an' stroppy. Sometimes yer think she'll bite yer 'ead off.'

'When are they moving in together?'

'Soon—once they've finished paintin'. Pete's tenants moved out last week. And I'm hoping to be back in me old flat next month as well—now the council have done it up.'

Lathom thought it wise to change the subject. He handed her a menu.

'What do you fancy?' he asked.

It was late afternoon before Lathom returned to his apartment block. He'd had a nice lunch with Michelle and was already growing very fond of her. There was so much of Jean in her, in the way she looked and her mannerisms, and also a little that reminded him of his own mother when she was young. It was still difficult to cope with the revelation that he now had a daughter and granddaughter—probably more so than the idea that he was now a vampire. He entered his apartment, his answering machine was flashing. Just one message—he'd been expecting this one for some time. He dialled the number and arranged to meet the next day.

Early the following morning, he polished his shoes, put on his best suit, put a 'Chow Mein' special in his coat pocket, collected his car from the resident's car park and drove through the Mersey Tunnel onto the Wirral. It was a short journey down the M53 to Chester but it brought back uncomfortable memories. He left the Chester bypass and drove through leafy suburbs, turning off Victoria Crescent and into Lower Park Road. The house was a short distance along on the left. He pulled into the gravel drive and parked alongside an old Jaguar. It was a substantial Victorian mansion surrounded by trees perched high on the hill overlooking the River Dee, the main city of Chester on its opposite bank. Placing his 'Chow Mein' special under the driver's seat, he walked to the front door. He hadn't been here for many years and the visit today was a bitter-sweet experience, an opportunity to reminisce with an old comrade but also an obligation to explain his actions. He checked his watch, waited until the prearranged time then knocked with the large brass door knocker—there was no bell—and waited. Even though he was on time he knew they would probably keep him waiting so as to keep him on edge.

After a few moments had passed, he knocked again. The door opened and a middle-aged blond man looked out at him. They recognised one another but did not acknowledge the fact. There was history between them. The middle-aged man stood aside to let him enter.

'He's in the garden—go straight through.' There was no eye contact.

Lathom knew the way. He walked through the house and out through the French windows into the garden. An old man was sitting in a wicker armchair, a blanket over his legs; he appeared to be watching the rowers on the river below. The old man turned as Lathom approached and indicated an uncomfortable looking cast iron chair to his side, and Lathom immediately felt like a schoolboy, summoned to the headmaster's study to explain his behaviour.

'So good of you to come Robert.' The old man looked at him through watery pale blue eyes.

'Always a pleasure sir. You're looking well.'

'Is it? Am I?—You were always a good liar, Robert.'

The old man looked over his shoulder and Lathom saw that they were being watched by the other man, who was now standing at the French window.

'John, a drink for Mr Lathom—whisky?'

'Tea.'

'You surprise me, Robert. They told me you were an alcoholic.'

Lathom shifted in his seat but said nothing.

The old man looked down at the river below. 'Did you row, Robert?'

'No sir, rugby was my sport.'

'Too short I suppose?'

He realised that he was being provoked to see how he would react. He still didn't understand how things would go and decided to let them play their hand first.

'You rather put the cat among the pigeons, Robert, by mentioning Operation Unicorn. We both know that no such operation ever happened—and if it did then the file has long since been *lost*. However, whoever took the call from your policeman typed in 'Unicorn' and the matter was referred to the top floor and then to me. A decision had to be made Robert, and it had to be made quickly.'

'Yes sir—thank you sir.'

'There is no need to thank me, Robert. I may have made the decision but it was not entirely an altruistic one.'

'No sir?'

'We had to balance the risks against the possible complications. Much as I would like to see you a free man, we cannot condone kidnapping and murder in an English city—even Liverpool.'

'No sir.'

'The fact that you'd mentioned Unicorn indicated to us that you intended to use it as a bargaining chip. We could of course have called your bluff—there's no file and no evidence—and you would have been convicted. Of course, you would have kept your mouth shut as you know we could easily obtain retribution even in Her Majesty's prisons. On the other hand—we had information that indicated that you might not make it to prison and, that if we called your bluff, you might see fit to give whatever information you had to foreign papers.'

'What information was that?'

'That you're an alcoholic with terminal cancer.'

'Ah.'

'I hope it was correct, Robert. We don't want you disappointing us and recovering—do we?'

'I thought it was because of my service to the department.'

The old man smiled. 'If only things could be so simple, Robert. Thank you for coming over for this little chat. You understand that the slate is now wiped clean? No more favours—understood?'

'Yes sir.'

The old man turned his head; the man at the French windows hadn't moved. 'Forget the tea, John—see Mr Lathom out.'

Lathom stood up. 'Goodbye sir.'

'Goodbye, Robert. I'll make sure that the department send flowers to your funeral.'

Lathom walked slowly back to his car.

'Bastard' he muttered, as he settled himself in the driver's seat then reached under the seat and took hold of the 'Chow Mein' special. He sat for a few minutes contemplating a return visit before he changed his mind. They might be expecting something of the sort. No doubt that was why the other man, John, had been watching from the French windows. Lathom decided to settle the score at a time of his own choosing, not theirs. In the meantime—if they were waiting for him to die they were going to have a long wait. He smiled, replaced the gun and was about to start the car.

'I wouldn't have died if you were sober.'

He turned and stared at a young woman sitting in the passenger's seat. She was quite pretty with short brown hair, she was wearing a frilly white blouse and a pleated skirt.

As she turned towards him, he could see that the opposite side of her face had been blown away by a gunshot.

'It was such a nice day for a picnic—not a day to die,' she continued unperturbed by the wound.

He took a deep breath. 'Look Sally, I know that you're all in my mind, but if it makes any difference, I'm sorry—I really am.'

She disappeared and he started his car, wondering how many more ghosts were out there, waiting to come back and remind him of his short comings. It was like being in his very own *Christmas Carol* except Dickens's ghost, Marley, had been replaced by dead lovers and colleagues. In the past, Lathom had been able to blot out his feelings and memories with alcohol, but now with immortality even that solace was denied him. He was beginning to realise that forever means exactly that: *for ever.*

He drove slowly back to Liverpool and his mind drifted back to the last time he had met Sally; a sunny Sunday nearly forty years before.

§

Lathom was feeling hung-over and slightly nauseous. They'd had a lock-in at the police club the night before and he hadn't got to bed until 2am. Now he was on a boring assignment with a young RUC officer, Sally Metcalfe. They were sitting in an unmarked police car, in a layby close to the border with the Republic of Ireland after a tip-off that the IRA were going to smuggle arms over the border in a furniture van. They had a description and the registration of the van and their job was to watch the road and to radio ahead when or if they sighted it. It would then be intercepted at a railway crossing a few miles further on. The general feeling in the squad was that it was probably a false lead and would be a waste of everyone's time, consequently Lathom was bored and spent the time trying to sleep off his hang-over.

He'd pushed the driver's seat back, reclined it and stretched out. It was a lovely spring day so he pulled down the sun visor to stop the sun shining in his eyes. He watched the road with little enthusiasm. They'd been there for four hours already and it had just been decided to give it one more hour then call things off. Sally, sitting alongside him, had angled the rear view mirror so that she could watch the road behind.

Their layby was in the middle of a long straight road in open countryside, the nearest village was five miles away and the traffic was particularly light at this time on a Sunday afternoon. The locals had been to church and were now either at home eating their Sunday roast or tucked up in the nearest pub. Lathom was hungry and looked forward to a meal and a 'hair of the dog' once they got back to base.

He and Sally were in a pea-green Morris Marina, and posing as a courting couple, which until recently hadn't been too far from the truth. They'd had an on-off relationship for a few months until she'd got bored with Lathom's drinking and gone back to her old boyfriend. The atmosphere in the car was a little tense which was partly the reason that Lathom was pretending to doze. Both were in plain clothes and, because it was a hot day, Lathom had taken off his coat and had therefore had to take off his shoulder holster and leave in on the back seat under his coat. Sally's gun was in her handbag at her feet. Their role was merely to act as early warning and they were in no danger and after so many hours' inactivity they had been lulled into a false sense of security. They'd eaten the sandwiches that they'd brought with them several hours before and Sally was just finishing the last *Kit-Kat*.

'Such a nice day for a picnic,' she said.

He grunted. In the distance he could see a motorcycle approaching. As it got closer he saw that it was small Honda moped, pale blue and cream, the type that looked like an Italian scooter but without the style. The rider who was perched on top of it was a large man with gold-rimmed sunglasses. He was wearing a silver crash helmet, a black rally-jacket with red and yellow stripes down the sleeves and large motorcycle gloves. Lathom thought he looked like an extra from a particularly naff version of *Easy Rider*.

The moped pulled into the layby in front of them. The man got off the moped, took a map from his coat and after staring at it for a few moments turned and walked towards their car.

'Bob?' Sally nudged Lathom in the ribs.

'Probably lost,' he said. He sat up in his seat and wound down his window. As the man approached Lathom noticed the shoes, they were shiny brown brogues, not the biker's boots he would have expected. He suddenly felt uneasy and reached under his seat for his gun—then realised that it was on the back seat.

He turned to get it then heard Sally shout, 'Bob!'

Lathom turned back to see the man pull a gun from under the map. Sally grabbed her gun from her handbag and as she levelled it the man fired through the windscreen. Lathom slid down his seat into the foot-well as bullets ricocheted around him.

He lay in the foot-well covered in broken glass and heard the moped racing away. Then all was silent. Sally lay across the passenger's seat. From where he crouched, she looked unharmed. He sat up and saw that a single shot had blown away the left side of her face. He was about to radio ahead then realised that this had been a well-planned ambush and by the time anyone responded the man would be long gone. He smashed out the remaining windscreen glass, started the engine and gave chase.

The moped had a head start; Lathom was squinting, partially blinded by the rush of air through the broken windscreen and by the sun which was low in the sky. Rounding a bend, the sun was obscured by trees and he was able to see the moped and its large rider a short distance ahead. Accelerating, he quickly closed the distance between them. The man must have seen something in his mirrors, turned, recognised Lathom's car and accelerated, crouching low over the handle bars like a jockey urging on a reluctant horse.

Lathom had expected the rider to pull over and fire at him then realised that he must have used all his bullets in the ambush. He was obviously trying either to reach safety or to draw Lathom into another ambush. Lathom decided to stop him —now.

He drew alongside the moped and swerved into its path. The moped and its rider flipped over and cartwheeled into a ditch by the side of the road; Lathom pulled off the road a little further on and switched on his hazard warning lights.

Anyone passing would think he had stopped due to his broken windscreen. He turned and, reaching under his coat on the back seat, retrieved his gun from his shoulder holster. Sally's body lay slumped against the passenger's door and he gently turned her head so that the bullet wound was shielded from view. It looked as though she was sleeping. After muttering some platitudes to her corpse, he cocked the gun and walked slowly back towards the moped.

The rider had obviously been injured in the crash and was limping badly. He was desperately trying to get into the cover of some trees a short distance from the road as Lathom ran towards him.

'Stay away you bastard or you'll get what she got!' shouted the rider, pulling out his gun and waving it at Lathom.

Lathom was unimpressed; he knew it was a bluff. He stopped and casually shot the rider in his good leg. The man screamed and fell to the ground, his gun falling from his hand. Lathom walked slowly up to him and stood over him. The rider was holding his leg and trying to stem the flow of blood.

'I've been bluffed by better then you—who set us up?' Lathom asked.

'Fuck off!'

Lathom pointed his gun at the rider: 'Last chance to be a hero.'

'Or what?'

'Tell me who—no one else will know. We'll take care of you. You'll go to prison as a hero for *the cause*, probably be out in ten years.'

The rider grimaced in pain and tried to laugh: 'Or what?'

'Or I blow off your balls,' said Lathom.

'Fuck off!'

Lathom pulled the trigger and the ground between the rider's legs exploded.

'Jesus!' the rider screamed then automatically grabbed his crotch.

'Need to adjust this sight,' said Lathom.

'OK! OK!…' The rider tried to push himself away from the hole in the ground. 'I tell you who and you won't make me testify?'

'Correct.'

'McMahon did it.'

'Superintendent McMahon?'

'Yeah—now call a fucking ambulance.'

'Why did he do it?'

'How the fuck should I know? I just know he did.'

'You don't know anything else?'

'No! Just get an ambulance. You said you'd take care of me.'

'I did—didn't I?' The rider nodded and Lathom shot him in the head exactly where he'd shot Sally Metcalfe.

He walked slowly back to the car and its silent occupant then radioed in to report. Half an hour later, a large-panel van recovered his car and the moped and a black transit van recovered the bodies. Lathom was taken to Belfast for debriefing. That evening the local television news reported that a Republican terrorist had ambushed an RUC patrol; an RUC officer, Constable Sally Metcalfe had been killed in the gun battle and the terrorist who was so far unidentified was also killed in the exchange of fire with other officers. The RUC were appealing for witnesses etc, etc… Whoever sent the man would assume he had died at the scene and that their secret was safely dead and buried.

The rider was soon identified as member of a local IRA battalion based over the border near Buncrana in the Republic, outside of British jurisdiction and therefore relatively safe for IRA members. The Garda tried to control their activities but, with few resources and many IRA sympathisers in the local population, the Garda was obliged to leave the IRA to operate relatively openly. It was even known that a local pub was their unofficial headquarters and that meetings were conducted there once a month.

The information regarding Superintendent McMahon was more difficult to confirm. It was common knowledge that there was a power struggle between the RUC and the Army and that Loyalist paramilitary organisations had infiltrated the RUC, but why would a loyalist give information to the enemy that resulted in the murder of a colleague?

The breakthrough came when they intercepted his telephone calls and found that he was being blackmailed. It appeared that he was bi-sexual and although married was having an affair with a young man, a typical 'honey pot' scam, such as the Russians often used. The young man was a Republican and had threatened to go to the papers claiming that McMahon had blackmailed him into having sex. McMahon's career and marriage would have been ruined. All his blackmailers said they wanted was to know which border crossing was going to be watched so that they could use another one to get the weapons into the North; he hadn't realised that they'd use this information to set up an ambush at the same time as they moved the weapons safely across the border thirty miles away. His calls to his ex-lover were becoming more and more desperate. It was obvious that he hadn't understood the implications of his betrayal.

It was decided not to arrest McMahon because that would alert the IRA. He was no longer considered a risk and would be safely spirited away with an early retirement—'due to ill health'—once they had settled the score. The ambush wouldn't be allowed to go unpunished. Something substantial needed to be done, something that would make the IRA think twice about flaunting their untouchable status over the border. Once he heard about this, Lathom made it known that he wanted to be involved and as a result he was called to a meeting in Belfast. It was to be a joint Army/ Special Branch operation and was given the code name, *Unicorn*.

§

A few days after his meeting in Chester, Lathom was waiting for the lift in his apartment building. He'd just had his follow-up appointment at the hospital and should have been in good spirits but something was troubling him.

'Hiya, Bobby.' Sheryl appeared alongside him holding a large designer carrier bag.

'Hi, Sheryl.' Lathom stared at his shoes; he seemed subdued.

The lift arrived with a 'ping' and he followed her inside. She pressed the button for the 13th floor. The door closed and now they were alone.

'What's up, Bobby?'

'Been to the Royal for my check-up.'

'And?'

'"Miraculous recovery," they said. They can't explain it… I'm not going to die after all.'

Sheryl giggled. 'Did you tell them why?'

'I said I'd become a vegan and a 'born again Christian'.'

'Did they believe you?'

'Who knows—but if I'd said I was a vampire they'd have sent me to the funny farm.'

'So why have you got a face like a wet weekend?'

'I'm going to have to leave Liverpool—soon, just when I'm getting to know Michelle and Natasha.'

'Why?'

'Some old friends of mine want to see me dead. When they find out that I'm not going to oblige them—they'll send someone to rectify the situation.'

'But, they can't kill you, Bobby.'

'No, but Michelle or Natasha will get caught up in it. It's safer for all concerned if I disappear as soon as possible.'

The lift 'pinged' and the door opened.

'Look Bobby, don't make any decisions yet.' Sheryl took hold of his arm. 'Come over for tea tonight and we'll talk it over—OK?'

Lathom nodded but said nothing.

That afternoon he began making plans for his disappearance. He sat at his kitchen table with a note book and scribbled notes then phoned and made an appointment to see a solicitor the following morning to draw up a will. He wanted to make sure that Michelle and Natasha would be well provided for. He'd leave them his cottage and the apartment. The bulk of his assets were still in his Swiss bank account and would be easy to access once he had a new identity. For the time being 'Geoff

Davies' would have to do—he had a passport in that name with a bank account and a full back-story. He'd spent time building an imaginary life for this alter ego many years ago. When he worked for the Department it was common knowledge that many people had taken similar precautions. You couldn't trust anyone—especially the Department; he'd learned that to his cost soon after being recruited from Special Branch.

The motto of the Department, MI5, was *Defende Regum,* 'Defend the Realm' but insiders joked it should be *Defende Rectum*—'look after your own arse'. Lathom took off his gold watch and turned it over, on the back was engraved *Defende Regum 1978-2008.* He laughed.

'So that's what you get for thirty years' service—a gold watch and a bunch of flowers on your coffin.'

He put the watch back on his wrist and continued with his plans for the future—and for his revenge. Switching on his laptop he started a new document and named it 'Operation Unicorn'. He began to type and the memories of that faithfully night nearly forty years before came flooding back.

§

Lathom was sitting in the back of a Wessex helicopter flown by an SAS pilot. It was night and everything was in darkness. The pilot was flying on instruments only. This was before night vision goggles and Lathom couldn't even see the face of the man opposite. How could they fly like this? Even though he couldn't see anyone clearly Lathom knew that there were six of them in the helicopter, all dressed identically: black balaclavas, green combat jackets and black gloves—the unofficial uniform of the IRA—and each man carried an Armalite assault rifle. The guns had come from an IRA arms shipment that had been intercepted the week before. They hadn't been handed in with the rest of the shipment and, because their serial numbers were concurrent, if recovered it would be assumed that they were IRA guns that had been successfully smuggled across the border.

The men in the helicopter were a mixed bag: Special Branch, regular Army and SAS. All were volunteers and all had a reason to be there. They were comprised of friends of Sally Metcalfe, ex-lovers or those with a grudge. Lathom was there on all three counts. The operation, although not officially sanctioned by the powers that be, was unofficially supported. It was commanded by an SAS Captain, Spalding.

Lathom resented Spalding who was everything he despised: good looking, well-connected and arrogant—perfect 'top brass' material. No doubt in twenty years he would be one of the chief of staff and this 'secret' escapade would be immortalised as a drunken anecdote. Whatever happened tonight, Lathom knew that Spalding would make sure that he received all the praise and that the others would suffer any criticism.

The plan was simple, perhaps too simple. The helicopter would cross the border and drop them on moorland a few miles outside Buncrana. This was a flagrant breach of Irish neutrality and could be considered an act of war if they were captured—which was why a blind eye had been turned to the preparations and they were all volunteers. If it failed, they would almost certainly face court-martials and/or prison sentences.

Three others had crossed the border the day before in stolen cars on false plates. The cars had all come from Belfast and were chosen to make it seem as though the operation was a power struggle between rival factions of the IRA. At that time, it was common for power struggles within the paramilitary organisations, be they republican or loyalist, to be resolved by violence—which was why they were dressed as IRA men and carried the appropriate weapons.

The helicopter touched down briefly with the rotor still spinning, leaving them just enough time to scrabble out through the door and drop onto the wet peat bog before if took off and roared back across the border. They stood ankle deep in the bog and listened to it disappear into the distance. Everything was black and silent.

Spalding checked his map by torch-light and took a compass bearing then indicated the direction to the rendezvous point. Half an hour later they were cold and wet and hiding in a disused barn close to the main road. An hour later the three cars arrived and they were divided between them. The journey to Buncrana took only twenty minutes but it was after eleven-thirty when they arrived. As it was mid-week, the streets were deserted.

They parked in a side street across the road from the pub which was brightly lit. The *Irish Rover* was a small ugly pub in a shabby part of town but intelligence had told them that the local IRA battalion was holding its monthly meeting there tonight. The pub should have been closed by now but there was obviously a lock-in going on inside as had been predicted. It had been decided to time the operation for this time of night because it was assumed that everyone would be drunk and any security would be lax. They pulled on their balaclavas and checked their weapons. The drivers kept the engines running and the six assassins crossed the road and lined up outside the two entrances to the pub. On Spalding's signal they kicked in the doors and burst inside. They were careful not to overlap their lines of fire, they were professionals after all and no one wanted to get caught in the cross fire. They emptied their magazines and reloaded. Before the alarm had been raised they were already in the cars and on their way to the border.

A minibus had been stolen the day before and hidden close to the border. They parked next to it and changed into civilian clothes, putting the uniforms and guns in the cars and set fire to them. It would be foolhardy to try and cross the border armed and everyone was under strict instruction to leave all weapons behind. They climbed into the minibus, put on football scarves and woolly hats, poured some beer on their clothes and scattered the empty cans on the floor of the bus. When they approached the Garda post at the border they were singing and appeared to be drunk and in good spirits. Spalding was sitting up front next to the driver and Lathom was in the seat behind him. As they pulled up to the check point the lone Garda officer walked up to the driver's window and knocked. The driver wound down the window.

'Evenin' officer. Yer havin' a quiet night?' asked the driver.

'So far—where yer goin' son?'

'Just back to Belfast. Cup match today—did you see it on the telly?'

The Garda officer grunted and shone his torch inside the bus at the occupants. His torch went from face to face, all young, all drunk. He was about to tell them to drive on when his torch stopped on the man sitting next to the driver, the man was taller and slightly older than the rest, and he seemed familiar. The Garda officer was sure he'd seen the face before; last month he'd been on one of those cross border co-operation courses with the British. Was this one of the IRA suspects whose photo he'd been shown?

The officer leaned into the bus through the open window and peered at the man intently then laughed and said, 'Captain Spalding, that's it—isn't it?'

The bullet caught him under the chin and the impact blew his hat and the back of his head off. He fell backwards onto the roadside. Spalding had shot from inside his coat with a pistol he should not have carried.

'Drive!' shouted Spalding.

The driver slammed the bus into gear and tore across the border.

Spalding turned to Lathom. 'You saw he was going for his gun? I had to do it—didn't I?'

Lathom said nothing; everyone in the bus was silent. The feeling of euphoria had evaporated with that single shot. They had killed tonight to avenge the death of a friend but Spalding had killed a friend to protect his career.

§

Lathom finished typing his summary of that night's events. Although it was almost forty years ago it still left a bitter taste in his mouth. Where was that bastard Spalding now? Probably in the House of Lords. Lathom smiled to himself: perhaps not for much longer though. He copied the file onto a disc. How many copies should he make, two or twenty? He'd decide tomorrow; one would do for now.

He looked at the pile of items in the corner of the room; he'd set aside things that might be useful to him in the future or that had particular significance to him. Since he hadn't decided how to disappear yet, the collection of things was rather random; if he was going to fake his own death then it would be important to leave many of his precious things behind so that any investigator wouldn't suspect it had been planned in advance, but if he just disappeared then he could take them with him or hide them away. Although in the latter case he would expect the department to come looking for him or, at the very least, to question his family. He had to balance the possible risks against his collector's instincts.

Among his treasure he had amassed a small personal armoury: Flanagan's Browning which Sheryl had taken from Kelly, the Glock pistol, handcuffs and Taser that he had taken from Kelly's thugs, plus Melville's Webley and his own 'Chow Mein' special with its silencer. No matter how he disappeared it was certain that he would need to be armed, but which could he take without arousing suspicion and which would he need to leave to throw them off the scent?

He put the 'Chow Mein' special and Flanagan's Browning to one side for sentimental reasons. He put the Webley in a second pile together with some of his books—he would give these to Melville. That left the *tazer,* handcuffs and the Glock. No one other than Kelly and his thug knew that he had them and they could be useful so he put them in a third pile for further consideration.

Next he looked at his photo albums. He would have loved to take them with him but that would give the game away, so he regretfully went to put them back on his bookshelf. Once the apartment had been searched they would be checked for clues to his disappearance and then returned to his family. He looked through them as he put them back and tried to commit the images to memory. Perhaps he could copy them? Would he have time? He'd make a final decision tomorrow. He was still arranging them on the shelf in chorological order when he kicked something hard under the bottom shelf and, bending down, retrieved the cutlass. He smiled remembering the time it had saved his life. He should really have got rid of it a long time ago because it linked him to the bodies in the River Severn but he decided to take it with him because no one other than Sheryl and Melville knew he owned it and even they didn't know about its history. So he placed it in the first pile together with the Browning and his 'Chow Mein' special.

He was starting to feel hungry again; it was nearly two hours since he'd last eaten. He checked his gold watch; it was almost five. Was it too early?

Just after five Lathom knocked at the door of the apartment opposite with a bottle of wine in his hand.

Sheryl opened the door.

'Oh—I thought you were Lee.' She seemed surprised.

'Sorry, shall I come back later?'

'No—come in,' She took the bottle from him, 'Lovely—I'll get the glasses; you take a seat.'

'Where's Lee gone?'

'Don't know, Bobby—He's hardly ever here at the moment.'

'You two OK?'

She shrugged. 'You tell me—I always joke about his wife and six kids in Toxteth but perhaps he really has got someone else.'

'Lee? No—really? I don't believe it.'

'I don't know, but I'm going to find out.'

'How?'

'I'm going to put an app on his phone so I can trace his movements.'

'You think that's fair?'

'All's fair in love and war, Bobby—isn't that what they say?'

'It's not because of me is it? I know Lee didn't want you to do it—but you saved me.'

'More *made* you than *saved* you.'

'Isn't it the same?'

'Not to Lee it isn't. He thinks being a vampire is a curse not a cure. He feels guilty that he's still alive and so many are dead. Some of them he loved but more because of all the ones he's killed.'

'What about you, Sheryl?'

'Me? It doesn't bother me. We've all got to die sometime and I've got an understanding with God.'

He still didn't understand what she meant about God. He took the computer disc out of his jacket pocket and threw it on the table. 'Look after that for me.'

Sheryl was curious, 'It's not a sex tape is it?' she giggled. 'You know me, I'm easily shocked.'

Lathom raised his eyebrows, and gave her a disdainful look. 'No—it is *not* a sex tape; for your information it's about *Operation Unicorn*. Can you look after it for me?'

'Yeah, course, Bobby—but why?'

'In case anything happens to me.'

'Such as?'

'In case I disappear—or have to disappear.'

The door slammed and Melville appeared.

'Hiya Lee, where've you been?' asked Sheryl.

He mumbled some excuse.

'Bobby's brought us a homemade sex tape,' she said.

Melville looked puzzled.

Lathom shook his head and silently mouthed, '*Ignore her.*'

Melville smiled and sat down next to Lathom. 'What is it then, Bob?' he asked.

'It's about a military operation in Northern Ireland in the 1970's that *didn't* happen.'

'Why have a record of something that didn't happen?'

'Because it *did* and Bobby was on it,' said Sheryl, '- and now someone wants to keep his mouth shut—permanently.'

'Exactly,' said Lathom, 'I couldn't have put it better myself.'

Sheryl smiled. 'Come and sit down you two—tea's ready,' she said. 'I've made loads of Scouse—Bobby's eating for four at the moment.'

Lathom told them about Operation Unicorn while they ate. When he'd finished they were silent for a while until Melville asked: 'What happened to Spalding?'

'The bastard got a commendation and a promotion. He was what we called a *Teflon* officer. Whenever the shit started flying none of it ever stuck to him—you know the sort.'

Melville nodded but he seemed preoccupied with his own thoughts.

'What about McMahon?' Sheryl asked. 'Did he get to retire?'

'Yes, for six months—then someone shot him one night in a multi-storey car park.'

'The IRA?'

'Or us—I don't know which.'

'Why?'

'He wasn't any use any more—to either side, and neither side wanted him to talk.'

'Is that why they want you dead too, Bobby?'

Lathom nodded, 'Any more Scouse left? I'm starving.'

It was just after eleven the following morning. Lathom had already been to see his solicitor and had drawn up his will; he'd had two breakfasts and was now sitting on a cast iron bollard by the side of Salt House Dock, eating a bag of chips. He was watching a large historic sailing ship negotiating the lock gates at Albert Dock. A small inflatable dingy had a line attached to its bow and it was using its outboard motor to gently pull the ship around and line it up with the entrance. A large herring gull landed on the cobbles next to him and, tilting its head on one side, studied him and his chips with its cold yellow eye.

'OK,' said Lathom, 'want a chip? Let's have a bet on who blinks first.'

He stared at the gull and the gull stared back. Its yellow eye was unblinking and seemed to be taunting him. He tried to distract it by waving a chip in his hand—but it ignored him and continued to hold his stare as though their eyes were joined by an invisible thread.

Eventually Lathom blinked, said, 'Oh bugger!' then threw a chip to the gull.

Rather than snatching at the chip laying on the cobbles in front of it, the gull slowly waddled over to it and, while maintaining eye contact with Lathom, picked it up in its beak, flicked it up in the air as though it were a fish, and swallowed it down in one. Lathom was about to applaud when something strange happened: the gull suddenly started retching, flapped its wings and regurgitated the chip.

'Jesus!' it said, 'I hate vinegar!' then it flapped its wings and flew off.

If it wasn't for his previous hallucinations Lathom would have been confused but he was getting blasé about them. He finished the rest of his chips, put the wrapper in the litter bin nearby and walked back towards his apartment where he saw Melville on the opposite side of the road. Lathom crossed the road. He wasn't sure if it was the right thing to do or not, but he felt uneasy about Sheryl tracking Melville's phone. He'd spent his life invading other's privacy and had found that it was rare for someone not to have something they'd prefer to keep to themselves. He felt responsible for the strain their relationship was under and didn't want to see it get out of hand. He really didn't believe that Melville had someone else; no doubt it was all a misunderstanding. He decided to tell him about the app so as to make him realise how upset Sheryl was. Perhaps they'd then patch thing up and he could stop feeling guilty.

Late the following morning, Sheryl had just returned to the apartment. She'd taken a taxi from the Cathedral after her chat with God; she and God had decided to give Melville the benefit of the doubt and she wanted to get back to the apartment before him. From what she'd seen this morning when she'd followed him to St Luke's it seemed that he was innocent after all; she really should start trusting him. She was sitting on the sofa looking at her phone. Melville's symbol was approaching the apartments; he was just walking past the Hilton and would soon be back home. Sheryl was beginning to feel ashamed for setting up the tracking app; it appeared that Lathom had been right all along and it was all in her mind. She went into the bathroom and touched up her make-up; she'd make him realise how much she loved him, try not be so hard on him all the time. She walked back into the lounge and checked the phone—the symbol hadn't moved. She went to the window and looked down to the street below—Melville was standing outside the Hilton with a woman. Sheryl went and got his military binoculars and studied her. The woman was blonde, probably mid-thirties and beautiful. Sheryl could see them talking, then he gave the woman a bouquet of red roses and they parted with a kiss. Melville walked towards the apartments and the woman walked in the opposite direction towards the Hilton Hotel.

By mid-morning the following day Lathom had already stubbed his toe on a pair of hair straighteners that had been left on the bathroom floor, he was beginning to regret letting Sheryl move in. He still had no idea what had happened yesterday. He'd met Sheryl leaving the apartment in tears, pulling her wheelie-case but she refused to tell him what had gone on between her and Melville, just that she was leaving the city. He'd persuaded her to stay at his apartment for the time being, reasoning that a reconciliation with Melville would be more likely if she was nearby. Lathom was sure that he was in some way responsible for them splitting up and felt duty bound to try and get them back together.

He'd tried to find out from Melville what had happened between them when he'd gone to pick up some of Sheryl's things, but Melville was equally perplexed so he'd told him to keep out of the way until he could find out what Sheryl was so upset about, then they could plan a successful reconciliation. Unfortunately, his plan appeared to have back-fired. Sheryl had now moved all her things into his apartment and, because she had many more clothes than he did, he'd insisted she have the master bedroom and en-suite bathroom. Now she was gradually taking over the other bathroom too. Lathom kicked the hair straighteners in frustration, forgetting that he was in bare feet; cursed again and clutched his foot.

There was a knock on the bathroom door.

'Will you be long Bobby? I need me straighteners.'

Lathom stormed out of the bathroom and sat down on the sofa in the lounge where a pile of Sheryl's things was propped against the bookshelves: a small backpack, a box of old photo albums and a hockey stick case.

Sheryl came back and plugged the straighteners into the socket next to him.

'Bathroom's free now, Bobby.'

'Didn't know you played hockey,' he grunted.

Sheryl gave him a puzzled look: 'I don't.'

He pointed at the hockey stick case.

She laughed, picked up the case and threw it to him. 'Want to give me your expert opinion?'

He unzipped the case, pulled out the package inside, unwrapped the silk shawl and stared at the two Japanese swords. 'Nice—very nice indeed.'

'Thought you'd like my girls.'

'Girls?'

'Yeah, Madame Butterfly and Puff.'

Lathom set the dagger to one side. The large sword had a black lacquer case and was decorated with gold butterflies, the intricate guard inlaid with silver. He withdrew the blade slowly and with reverence and it made a sound of such quality and perfection that he imagined that that was what the door of God's walk-in wardrobe would sound like: 'sssh.'

He studied the blade with an expert's eye.

'Tang dynasty?' he asked and Sheryl nodded. He re-sheathed the blade then turned to the silver dagger, which he examined as carefully. The scabbard was beautifully engraved with a fierce oriental dragon.

'OK, I understand Madame Butterfly—but why Puff?'

Sheryl laughed. 'Don't you remember the song?'

'What song?'

'Puff the magic dragon.'

They both laughed.

'Where did you get them?' he asked. 'They should be in a museum you know.'

'A friend gave them to me.'

'Wish I had friends like that. You realise how much they're worth?'

'Its only money Bobby—some things are more important.'

'What happened to your friend?'

'Someone chopped his head off.'

'Who?'

'Me.'

'Why?'

'He asked me to—isn't that what friends are for?'

'But—why? Why did yo…?'

'Sorry Bobby love to chat—gotta go—havin' me nails done in ten minutes.' She leaned over and kissed him on the top of his head, grabbed her handbag and was gone leaving him to stare at the swords before carefully re-wrapping them in the shawl. Perhaps he wouldn't complain about the mess in his apartment; he'd prefer to keep his head where it was.

Sheryl called the lift and, while she waited, watched the floor indicator count up from the ground floor, she asked herself yet again—why had Melville lied to her? She'd seen him take flowers to St Luke's, then she'd seen him meet up with the woman in red. Why make-up a story about an old woman called Dora? Perhaps he'd seen her following him and taken the flowers to the memorial to throw her off the scent but arranged to meet the other woman later when he knew that Sheryl wasn't watching him. That was no doubt why he had been surprised to find her back at the apartment when he returned; that must be it. She checked the floor indicator again:

10… Why hadn't he come to see her last night and told her the truth? He knew how upset she was, that was the least he could do. Lathom said that he'd told Melville to stay away but she didn't believe him.

11… No, he was probably too ashamed to face her. He must realise that she'd seen him with that woman and got Lathom to lie for him, to give him time to concoct some story. She should go and hammer on his door, get him to tell her the truth.

12… He should behave like a man and own up to his affair, then they could both move on; admit their relationship was a mistake. It wasn't natural for vampires to live together. Perhaps it was time for her to move on?

13… 'Ping' the door opened and there was Melville, standing in the lift and looking at his feet. He stepped out of the lift before he saw her and seemed confused. Her resolved failed her and she pushed past him, quickly closing the lift door behind her.

The lift seemed to descend too quickly and she was still drying her eyes when the doors opened at the bottom. Why did she always fall in love with the tragic ones? Perhaps next time she should try a bastard—it'd be so much simpler. She hurried across Chavasse Park to her appointment at the beautician's but her mind was in another time and place. She hadn't thought about Charlie for years. Now the more she thought about him the more he reminded her of Melville. Why was that? They weren't at all alike. Perhaps it was to do with guilt?

She'd had her nails done then decided on impulse to have a few minutes on the sunbed. These days she usually had a spray tan, but it wasn't as if the UV was going to kill her was it? She lay under the bright tubes with the small dark glasses protecting her eyes and imagined she was on a foreign beach. She could feel a warm glow as she gently tanned and was daydreaming about a tall handsome stranger holding a large cold cocktail when a long buried memory rose to the surface of her mind.

§

Sheryl, or Sharleen as she then was, was driving along a dusty road deep in the red centre of Australia's outback.

She'd decided to drive rather than fly on the off chance of picking up a 'hot date' along the way. The radio of her hired Holden was tuned into a country station and she was singing along to a Dolly Parton song. The air-con was on maximum and she was making good time on the journey to Darwin. She'd been driving for four days so far with another three to go and this section of the road was particularly isolated—it was over sixty miles to the next town. The car started to pull to one side and she realised that she had a puncture. Coming to a stop, she stood by the side of the road, cursed and then kicked the tyre. She checked the boot, found the spare and the car-jack and was about to start changing the wheel when she saw a car approaching through the heat haze. Why sweat, she thought, when she could try her damsel in distress routine. The car approached and she stood looking helplessly at the flat tyre being careful to show plenty of leg.

The car drew nearer and she saw that it was actually an old pick-up driven by a young man with blond curly hair.

'Bingo!' she thought. 'A tyre changer and a 'hot date' all in one.'

As the car stopped next to her, she wiped away an imaginary tear and pouted at the driver who wound down his window. Suddenly, she 'sensed' him—and his look showed that he 'sensed' her two.

'Where are you going, *sister*?'

'Darwin.'

He pointed at the wheel.

'You going to change that or am I?'

'What with these nails?'

He laughed. 'Get in the cab and keep cool and I'll soon have you on your way.'

She watched him changing the wheel. He was young, perhaps early twenties, with a stocky muscular frame and short curly blond hair. His skin was heavily tanned and he wore old khaki shorts and a faded plaid shirt. He finished changing the wheel put away the punctured tyre and shut the boot, then he tapped on the window and she wound it down,

'OK—all done. Have a good journey.'

'Is there a motel nearby?' She knew there wasn't.

'Not nearby—about sixty odd miles.'

'You live near?'

'Yeah, ten miles back where you've come from, then another five off the highway in the bush.'

'Can I stay with you?' She smiled her most inviting smile.

He laughed. 'OK—but just for tonight.'

She stayed two years.

'Poor Charlie,' she thought. 'Always so guilty- never truly happy. That black cloud was never far away.'

Charlie, or Charles Edwin Sinclair had been born in Oxfordshire in 1893. He'd volunteered at the outbreak of war and been posted to the Middle-East. By April 1915, he was sheltering from Turkish snipers in a small dugout below the heights of Gallipoli when the naval barrage began from the British fleet in the bay. There were about ten people in the dugout, most from his regiment and a scattering from others who had been separated from their units in the confusion of battle. The shells landed on the Turkish positions and his commanding officer tried to rally the men for another assault under cover of the naval bombardment. Charlie always felt safe when his commanding officer was near. Captain Bellingham was one of those people who seemed untouchable. He never showed any sign of fear and was always the first out of the trench. Bellingham rounded up his small group and they cautiously left the dugout and crouched low in the shallow trench ready to advance on the Turkish positions. They'd fixed their bayonets and Bellingham had drawn his revolver when he realised that he'd left his binoculars in the dugout and asked Charlie to fetch them.

Charlie was about to enter the dugout when there was huge explosion. One of the fifteen-inch shells had misfired and fallen short. It landed just behind the trench and he was thrown forward by the force of the explosion into the dugout, which collapsed on top of him. When he regained consciousness, everything was black and his ears were ringing and he had to dig himself out of the soil and rubble, covered in blood and with shrapnel wounds in his back—but other than those wounds he seemed unharmed. Where the trench had once been there was a huge crater. He pulled off his blood-soaked shirt and examined his wounds which seemed too superficial to account for the amount of blood on his clothing and it was only then that he realised that it wasn't his blood; this was all that remained of his friends and Bellingham. Charlie was the only survivor. The other soldiers called it 'the luck of the Devil' and said that he must have a guardian angel—he even believed it for a time.

Then the dreams began.

At first he thought that the dreams and hallucinations were the result of shell-shock. The medics thought so too and eventually he was repatriated to England.

The next thing Sheryl knew for certain was that he was in China when the Japanese invaded, working as an aid worker for a Christian mission. He'd witnessed first-hand the atrocities, the mass rapes and the civilians hacked to death or buried alive. As a foreign national he was safe but the Japanese military found him an embarrassment and he was soon deported.

He went to Hong Kong to work with refugees and, when war was declared, signed up and was posted to Singapore. When Singapore fell to the Japanese he was soon on the route march to a prison camp and then onto work on the Death Railway.

Charlie would never talk in detail about the next three years. He carried a deep sense of guilt for what took place. Somehow, while his fellow prisoners were beaten or starved to death, he remained healthy. He gradually began to realise what had happened to him in that trench in Gallipoli. He knew that the other prisoners talked behind his back, thought that he provided information to the Japanese in exchange for extra food or that he was stealing it from the sick. As they became thinner and more malnourished his health seemed more and more obvious; no one trusted him and he felt as though he was in two prisons at once.

After the war he went to Japan to try and reconcile present realities with what he had seen. Instead of a Military dictatorship he found a warm welcome from an impoverished population. He taught English to the orphans and learned much of their history and culture and was saddened to see how the Samurai principles of honour and chivalry had been twisted and abused by the military in order to excuse their atrocities. He used his money to purchase items from the destitute inhabitants and, when he eventually left, he took these precious items with him to Australia.

Like all vampires, by that time he'd discovered that he needed to keep moving before people noticed that he failed to age, or else they began to ask too many questions about his past and the occasional missing person. When Sheryl had stumbled into his life that day in the outback, he'd been living on this isolated sheep station for ten years. He had a well for water, a generator for electricity and an ample supply of vegetable which he grew for himself, plus lamb, beef and goat meat from his livestock. He had no use for the outside world and had turned his back on mankind after the dreadful things that he had seen and experienced.

It was only after she'd been there a few weeks that she discovered that he suffered with depression. Whether it was something he'd always had or was the result of his experiences she had no way of knowing. He'd stopped taking blood some time before, partially due to necessity—there was no one within eighty miles—but mainly due to guilt; Charlie felt guilty to have survived when so many had died and died in appalling ways. He thought that vampires were parasites, exploiting the weak and defenceless, felt that the world would be a better place without them—especially without him.

By the time Sheryl discovered all this she was already in love with him and hoped that her love would make him change his mind, and, for a while, it seemed to help. She couldn't persuade him to take blood again so, out of necessity, she would leave for a few days every few months. He would drive her the eighty miles to the railway station and she would take a train somewhere. A few days later she would return with a clear conscience and another police force would be searching for a missing person. He never asked where she went or what she did and she never explained.

The longer he went without blood the more morose he became and his depression deepened. He started drinking and he was often drunk. One night when he was very drunk and couldn't sleep, he told her how he'd tried to kill himself many times before. He described shooting himself and poisoning himself, both to no avail, how he'd jumped from a tall building—but survived. As he spoke she realised that he would try again and, no matter how much she loved him, it would always be this way.

After one particularly difficult week, she decided that she needed to get away and he drove her to the station but when she returned a few days later he wasn't there to meet her. She had a feeling that something was wrong and, after hiring a car, drove back to the sheep station. As she turned off the main road onto his track she could already smell smoke. She rounded the last bend and saw the ruins of the farmhouse. The smell of charred timber was much stronger now. The body of his dog lay on the porch; it had been shot at close range. She tried to open the front door but the fire had welded it to the frame and when she pushed harder the frame splintered and the door fell off its hinges. Charlie was lying next to his shotgun, horribly burned but still alive.

He tried to speak but his lips were scorched and swollen and his features had been burned away. He lifted his hand and she saw that he'd lost most of his fingers. An empty petrol can lay next to the fireplace. It was obvious that he had killed his dog then tried to blow up the house and himself. He was trying to point and she realised that he was pointing towards the barn. He was wheezing and trying to speak. She leaned close to his face, tears on her cheek as she tried to understand him.

She ran to the barn. Inside was a small pile of her things and something wrapped in a silk shawl. She unwrapped his swords—then realised what he wanted from her. That evening she buried his body with his dog on the hill above the farm. Then loaded her belonging into the hire car and headed north for Darwin.

§

The timer of the sunbed buzzed and bright light cut off. Sheryl sat up and took off the dark glasses and was surprised to find her cheeks wet with tears. She picked up the towel she'd been resting her head on and dabbed her eyes.

'Poor Charlie—at least you got what you wanted.' she sniffed, 'Why can't I?'

She dressed and went to pay, as she handed over her credit card the cashier noticed she had been crying and asked, 'What is it luv—man trouble?'

'Yeah—sort of,' she sniffed.

'Pretty thing like you—don't go losing your head over some lad.'

Sheryl smiled. 'Don't worry—I won't.'

She walked back towards the apartment block. She'd let Melville sweat for a few days, then perhaps he'd come clean and explain about that woman in red. After that, perhaps it would be time to move on again; she couldn't stay with Bobby for much longer and she wouldn't look for another apartment nearby. She had no wish to share this city with Melville and his new woman. At least, now she was single she wouldn't have his guilt to deal with and she could start looking for more 'hot dates'; perhaps it wouldn't be so bad after all. Sheryl decided to celebrate her freedom by going out clubbing that evening. Now she'd had her nails done, it seemed a shame to sit at home moping while Melville and his woman were probably out enjoying themselves.

Melville was in Lathom's apartment drinking a coffee.

'The thing is, Bob, I don't know what I've done.'

'Just apologise.'

'I've tried that—she ignored me.'

'Buy her some flowers or chocolates and a soppy card, women love that sort of thing. Then you'll get her back and I'll get my apartment back.' He kicked the hair straighteners on the floor beside him.

'If you think I'll work …'

'Come over later tonight and surprise her.'

'Can't Bob, I've got an appointment. Can I leave flowers and a card this afternoon?'

'Drop them off whenever you like, but I'm working on the tug later. You need a key?'

Melville nodded. 'Sheryl took the one you gave us.'

'I've got one in my overalls in the car. Come down to the car park and I'll give it to you before I go out.'

They took the lift down to the car park, Lathom carrying a bag of clothes that he'd brought back from his cottage that he intended to take to a charity shop and Melville carrying a pile of books for him. Lathom's car was parked in the next bay to Melville's Range-Rover.

As they reached the car Lathom rummaged in his pocket for his car key-fob and pressed it. There was a 'peep' and the doors unlocked.

'Put the books on the back seat, Lee.'

Lathom went to open the driver's door but, with his arms full, he dropped the keys. As he bent down to pick up his keys, he saw a small pile of dried mud on the floor under the car—instantly, he froze and shouted.

'Lee—don't open the door!'

'Why?'

Lathom knelt down and looked under the car. 'Bastards,' he muttered. He reached underneath, and carefully removed a package wrapped in silver gaffer tape. It was about the size of a bag of flour. He put it on the car roof and it made a 'clunk' noise as though attracted to the metal.

'Magnetic,' he said.

'Magnetic what?'

'Bomb—retirement present from some old colleagues.'

'What do we do now?'

'Nothing—it's safe now.' Lathom indicated a wire attached to it. 'They probably wired it into the ignition, but you can just as easily plug it into a mobile, it works just as well. You call the phone, it makes the circuit—and *BOOM !!'*—"Goodbye Robert been nice knowing you."'

'Will they try again?'

'Bound to. They'll probably leave it a while, hoping that I use the car. If that doesn't work, then they'll get someone I know to call me and ask me to come and see them urgently.'

Lathom opened the door and searched his overalls for his spare apartment key. He handed it to Melville together with the bomb.

'Can you look after it for me?'

Lathom put the bag for the charity shop on the back seat and picked up his overalls and they walked back to the lifts in silence; Lathom deep in thought. He took the lift to the ground floor while Melville returned to his own apartment, left the bomb on the kitchen work surface and collected his coat and wallet. He checked his watch; he had just have enough time to buy flowers and bring them back before his appointment but he decided not to leave them in Lathom's apartment until later, when he knew Sheryl was in and he could explain everything properly.

Sheryl returned to Lathom's apartment; there was no sign of him, then she remembered that he was working on the tug restoration that afternoon. She'd expected to have heard something from Melville though, even a card or some flowers would be a start.

'Sod him,' she thought, 'plenty more fish in the sea.' She began to plan what she would wear tonight.

It was just after seven when Lathom got back. He'd lingered for a drink with Owen from the tug preservation society to give Sheryl and Melville some time alone to sort things out, but Sheryl was alone on the sofa sorting through her handbag. Her trusty penknife and phone on the coffee table in front of her.

'Hiya, Bobby—just off out. I've left you some tea in the fridge, just heat it up.'

He looked around. 'Any sign of Lee?'

'Why?'

'Nothing—just curious.'

She tucked her penknife into her bra, dropped her mobile into her handbag and stood up. She kissed Lathom on the cheek as she made for the door.

'Don't wait up,' she said.

Lathom switched on the kettle. Normally he'd have reached for his whisky but it no longer provided any comfort. He microwaved his meal and was about to sit down and watch a documentary when there was a knock at the door and there was Melville, holding a large bouquet of flowers and wearing one of the colourful shirts that Sheryl had bought for him and that Lathom privately knew he hated.

'Too late,' said Lathom.

'Sorry?'

'She's gone out. There's a programme on about the Zulu War, you can tell me if it's accurate or not—or are you off to the Rio Carnival?'

Melville shrugged, and handed him the flowers and the card.

'Can you give these to her Bob? Tell her I called to apologise.'

Melville returned to his own apartment and Lathom put the flowers and card on the side and continued sorting through his belongings, deciding what to leave and what take with him. He'd already booked a flight, for the following day. Once he was out of the country it would be much easier to fake his own death and throw them off the trail. He had two passports: for Robert Lathom and Geoff Davies. He'd fly out as Lathom and then use the Davies identity to start a new life. The only thing he couldn't predict was how long they'd give the bomb to work before they decided to have another try at killing him.

By midnight he'd selected the few things that he would take with him, too many and they'd smell a rat. He'd copied all the research for his book on the King's Regiment onto a memory stick together with some of his precious photographs.

He knew that after his disappearance the police and then his ex-colleague would search the apartment. They'd look for clues on his computer; so he'd take that with him and dispose of it discretely. The photo albums would eventually be given back to Michelle when they'd made sure that they were of no use. He checked his watch—still no sign of Sheryl. Well, he wasn't going to wait up for her; she could look after herself. He went to bed.

He'd been asleep for a few hours when his phone began to ring. He cursed; it was probably Sheryl or Lee—who else would be ringing at this time?

'What now?' Lathom was angry.

'Bob? It's Danny, Danny Corcoran—can yer cum over an' see us now? It's urgent like.'

Lathom tried to sound surprised and angry. 'OK Danny, if it won't wait until morning—give me an hour or so.'

He hung up the phone and went to get dressed.

St Luke's

Melville was still angry. He couldn't believe what Bob had told him yesterday: that Sheryl had put an app on her phone so that she could track his movements. OK, so he'd now done the same but he wasn't going to use it for that reason; he'd just done it to see how she'd like it. When she eventually owned up, he would too. Actually that wasn't true; when she owned up, he'd feign surprise. It wasn't as though he was doing anything to be ashamed of. He always went for a walk in the morning; he'd tell her exactly where he went if she asked. He'd left Sheryl in bed apparently fast asleep, left the apartment by the side door and cut through Chavasse Park and on through the city centre towards Central Station. He planned to do something this morning that he knew Sheryl would disagree with because she wanted him to leave the past behind and move on, but perhaps he wasn't quite ready for that just yet. He was buying flowers from the stall opposite Central Station when he wondered if the app worked in the apartment. He knew that mobiles didn't work very well due to the mass of concrete and thick double-glazing; would the app still show Sheryl tucked up in bed? While he waited for the florists to wrap up the bouquet, he switched on the app and was surprised to notice that Sheryl's symbol wasn't at the apartment block as he had assumed but on the other side of the street. He casually turned around as if apparently watching a busker and saw her hiding in a shop doorway pretending to window shop. He nearly laughed out loud—it was a bookmaker's. So she'd decided to follow him had she? Well he'd probably have told her about this afterwards anyway but at least now she'd know he was telling the truth. He paid for the flowers and walked slowly up Bold Street deep in thought. He decided not to write a card to go with the flowers; he knew who they were for so there was no need.

At the top of the street a church was silhouetted against the bright blue sky. From this distance it looked like any other church but he knew that its appearance was deceptive. This was St Luke's or, as the locals referred to it, 'the bombed out church'. The blitz of 1941 had left it an empty shell but Melville remembered it for another reason—this was Charlotte's church.

Today was her birthday. How old would she be? One hundred and twenty-six, he calculated. He stood in the churchyard but there were no gravestones. He now knew that she hadn't committed suicide as he'd once thought; Kelly had murdered her for revenge. He placed the flowers on a memorial to the dead of the Irish Potato Famine, which would have to do because he had no idea where she was buried, then he stood in silence for a few moments. There was no need for words. How many other lovers had he buried?

Sheryl said *mortals* were like goldfish: lovely to look at, but don't get too fond of them because they never last long. Perhaps she was right, perhaps he should stop trying to live like *them*; just do what she did, do what came naturally without the guilt and recriminations. It would certainly be simpler. The blood always made him feel energised. Why didn't he just embrace the way he was, the way he'd been *made* by Isabella two hundred years ago? He was certain that Isabella hadn't felt any guilt for that so why should he feel so guilty about all his 'Emmas'? His guilt surely couldn't go back to the first one; that had been accidental, something that happened while he was still disorientated by his hallucinations and was not responsible for his actions. Melville found that he could only remember brief snatches of that fateful night. After all these years he found it difficult to visualise exactly what Emma had looked like, or indeed Isabella's husband whom he had also murdered in the alley. Why didn't he feel guilty for the husband's death? Perhaps it was because he had killed men before but that was the first time he'd killed a woman—a child. He closed his eyes and concentrated hard. He could almost see Emma's face, small thin and blonde, but then another image took her place—Isabella. There was no forgetting *her*, he could almost hear her voice. He opened his eyes and was immediately back in the present. An old Chinese woman was standing and staring at him then she turned and walked towards the church in silence. He heard music coming from inside and, in order to dispel his melancholic mood, decided to investigate further.

Sheryl stood on the far side of Leece Street. She'd followed Melville up Bold Street, but why? Was she really so insecure about their relationship? Perhaps she'd been alone for too long and no longer trusted anyone else? Perhaps it went back to being abused her step-dad? All she knew was that she needed to know that he wasn't keeping anything from her, needed to trust him implicitly if their relationship was going to survive. She knew that he was still haunted by his past and was finding it difficult to let go of his guilt and move on, and that making Lathom a vampire had put an additional strain on their relationship. Sheryl crossed the road and peered over the cast iron railings of the church. Melville was kneeling; he placed the flowers on a memorial then stood up and walked into the church itself. Now she understood. She felt ashamed to have doubted him. She turned and walked away—time to have another chat to God.

Melville entered the church. St Luke's had been preserved as a memorial to those killed in the Blitz. The incendiary bombs had destroyed the roof and all the woodwork and all that remained was a hollow stone-and-brick shell, now used for open-air concerts and public events. He entered through the stone archway. There was music playing and a keep fit class were assembling inside the walls, a strange miscellaneous collection of people, young and old, fit and obviously unfit. The old Chinese woman took off her coat, folded it carefully and set it to one side. She wore a tracksuit underneath. The instructor clapped her hands and the class lined up in three irregular lines. There was a gap in the front rank next to the Chinese woman and she waved Melville into the space. He found himself complying, more out of embarrassment than out of any desire to exercise, but once they began he realised that it was a Tai Chi class and relaxed. It'd been many years since he'd last done this but the familiarity of the moves was comforting. Soon his surroundings melted into the background and the hypnotic sensation of the moves took him to a different time and place. Suddenly Melville realised that the music had stopped and that everyone else was staring at him. He had obviously continued after the music had finished. He was embarrassed and tried to leave but the old Chinese woman took hold of him by his arm.

'Stay—that was most enlightening. Who was your teacher, young man?'

'Yang Luchan,' he answered without thinking.

She laughed. 'No—not which school of Tai Chi …Yang Luchan died in the 19th century.'

He recovered himself and made up a name. The woman gave him a questioning look but did not pursue it.

'What's your name, young man?

'Melville, Lee Melville.'

'Well, Mr Melville will you give me your arm? I find that this exercise has provoked my arthritis. My hips may be artificial but this dodgy knee is definitely still mine and would appreciate a strong young arm for support.'

Melville smiled and linked arms with her. His momentary embarrassment had passed. They walked slowly out of the grounds, she was limping slightly. He hadn't noticed that when he'd followed her inside.

'Would you mind walking me home, Mr Melville? I live only a short distance from here and shall not detain you for too long.'

He felt relaxed in her company and happy to have something to take his mind off the past or indeed the present. They walked slowly down Berry Street towards the Chinese Arch and China Town.

'What did you think when you first saw me Mr Melville? Did you think I was just another old Chinese woman, perhaps a cleaner or a cook in a restaurant? You can be honest—we all make value judgements based on first impressions and rarely are they entirely correct.'

Melville smiled. 'Yes, I suppose I did.'

'A generation before my own you would have been correct. My mother was a cook and a cleaner, although Irish and not Chinese. My father was from Shanghai, a merchant seaman; he gave me this skin and his surname, but little else.'

'Why?'

'He survived the German U-boats but could not overcome institutional racism.'

'Sorry?'

'Once the War was over, they had no use for foreign seaman. The police came and rounded them all up and deported them to China. My brother was three and my mother was six months pregnant with me. They were married but that made no difference.'

'What happened to him then?'

'No one knows; they all disappeared. Perhaps the communist government imprisoned them or shot them as spies. It was a difficult time after the War; old friends became new enemies and vice versa.'

'Aren't you bitter about it?'

'Why? Perhaps he didn't want to come back, perhaps he had another family and lived a long and happy life. I hope he did; I prefer that idea to a labour camp and a firing squad.'

'Surely you must be angry about it?'

'Mr Melville, I was once angry about everything. I was a radical; I marched for Nuclear Disarmament, marched against Apartheid; I even burned my bra on the steps of St George's Hall—not something I shall be doing again.'

Melville laughed. She smiled and continued.

'I've been divorced twice, out-lived both husbands and one son, my hips are artificial as are my teeth. I have little time for anger and less for grief. Flowers are wasted on the dead, Mr Melville—give them to the living.'

He remembered that she'd watched him place the flowers on the memorial, and felt his melancholy returning. They walked in silence for a few moments, each with their own thoughts.

'What did you think of me—when you first saw me?' Melville asked eventually.

'I thought you were what my mother would call *an old soul*, Mr Melville, someone who seems to have experienced more than their years. You have the look of someone who has suffered and who can't let go of the past.'

Melville said nothing. Before they reached China Town she turned left and they walked slowly up the hill stopping outside a smart Victorian terrace, Hope Place.

'Do you love her?' she asked, turning towards him.

'Who?'

'The girl that you've been thinking about, Mr Melville?'

'How do you kno-?'

She raised an eyebrow. He laughed.

'Yes.'

'Then tell her! Buy her red roses and tell her. Leave your grief with the dead and look after the living.'

'I will—I know you're right.'

'I always am. Mr Melville—do you play chess?'

'Not very well.'

'Excellent, I always prefer to win. You know where I live—I shall expect a visit.'

'I don't even know your name.'

'Professor Wong, but you, Lee, may call me Dora.'

Melville agreed to return. As he began to walk down the hill, she called after him.

'Remember—red roses.'

He waved and walked slowly towards the city centre, deep in thought. He knew that what she'd said was true, that he should forget about the past. What good did this grieving do, other than stop him enjoying the present? He should concentrate of the present and leave the dead and his past lives firmly in the past. He thought of Sheryl and on impulse opened his phone to see where she was. He felt uneasy about spying on her and smiled as he realised that she could well be doing the same to him.

Her symbol was alongside the Catholic Cathedral, 'Paddy's Wigwam', no doubt she was having a chat with God again. He wondered if the chat was about him this time. He checked his watch and calculated that he'd have time to buy the flowers and get back to his apartment before she returned. He closed his phone and headed towards the flower stall near Central Station once again.

Fifteen minutes later he had bought a dozen red roses and was walking back through the shopping mall with a spring in his step. He'd tell Sheryl how much she meant to him and promise to be more open in the future, he would try to forget about the past and stop feeling guilty about giving in to his desires. Melville was just walking past the front entrance to the Hilton Hotel and was checking his watch—he'd just have time to put the flowers in a vase before Sheryl returned—when he heard a woman calling someone's name. He ignored it; she wasn't calling him. The voice grew louder and closer.

'Richard!'

Melville carried on walking he didn't look around.

'Richard—is that really you?' A woman grabbed him by the arm and stopped him in his tracks. He turned and tried to explain that he wasn't called Richard that she was mistaken.

She was probably in her early thirties, blonde and attractive, dressed in red with a brown fur coat draped over her shoulders. Her grip on his arm was strong and she showed no intention of releasing it.

'Richard?' she stared at him intently, 'it is you—why are you ignoring me?'

'I'm sorry—you're mistaken; my name isn't Richard; it's Lee.'

'Don't you recognise me Richard? I know it's been an eternity but have I really changed that much?'

Melville looked again and suddenly the years fell away and he was standing on a street in Brussels two hundred years before. He had rehearsed what he would say in this situation many thousands of times before. He would be friendly and courteous, hide his true feeling—hide the pain. But now suddenly his mind was a blank and he floundered for a response, after a long pause the best he could do was mutter.

'Isabella?'

She smiled and let go of his arm. 'I knew you recognised me—you were just teasing. Was it to punish me Richard? I know that I deserve it.' She pouted. 'But I have regretted leaving you every single day since then. I've cried myself to sleep and thousand times.'

'Isabella?' Melville was still stunned. She was impatient.

'Yes, yes—I'm still Isabella. Why are you calling yourself Lee? Richard is such an aristocratic name; Lee is so … ordinary.'

'I like Lee.'

'No matter, it can easily be changed.' She seized the bouquet: 'red roses—you remembered.'

'Erm, no I'm sorry they were for -.'

She stood on her tip toes and kissed him on the cheek.

'Meet me in the Hilton foyer tomorrow morning at ten.'

Then she was gone. All the certainty he had felt a few minutes before had now evaporated; he'd wanted to put the past behind him but now it had become the present. He shook his head and walked slowly towards the apartment. He'd have to tell Sheryl about it when she returned, then try and keep the two of them apart; somehow he couldn't see them getting along. In fact, on further consideration, it would be better if Sheryl didn't find out at all. He'd meet Isabella tomorrow and explain that there was no future for them, explain that he loved Sheryl. Perhaps Isabella was just passing through, and once she'd left the city he could explain everything to Sheryl without the risk of a blood bath.

He took the lift to their apartment; he wanted to have time to collect his thoughts before Sheryl arrived home. But when he unlocked the door he heard the TV in the lounge. Sheryl was sitting on the sofa filing her nails. She looked up as he kissed her on the cheek.

'Hiya Lee, where've you been?'

'Just for a walk.'

'Did you meet anyone on your *walk*?'

He thought he detected something in her tone of voice, hesitated and then replied, 'No—why?'

Sheryl pushed him to one side and ran out of the room. He didn't understand what was going on and followed her into the bedroom where she was bundling clothes into her wheelie-case and crying at the same time.

'What's the matter?' he asked.

'As if you don't know Lee… you went to the florist and then met another woman. Who is she?' She shut the suitcase and stood up staring at him, tears streaking her cheeks.

He smiled, relieved; she must have seen him earlier this morning at St Luke's.

'Oh, that was Dora.'

'No more lies Lee, is she your girlfriend?' Sheryl sniffed and wiped her eyes on her tracksuit sleeve.

'Hardly—she's not my type and after all she must be nearly seventy.'

Sheryl slapped his face hard and stormed out of the room dragging her wheelie-case behind her.

'What was that for?' He tried to follow but she slammed the door in his face.

He sat on the sofa; perhaps she would calm down later and return. It certainly wasn't a suitable time to mention Isabella if she reacted that way about him talking to an old woman in a graveyard. An hour later there was a knock at the door; he thought it would be Sheryl and that she must have forgotten her key, but when he opened it, it was Lathom.

'Come to get her things.' He held up a piece of paper, 'I've been given a list.'

'Where is she?'

'She's moved in with me—didn't think I could refuse after what she's done for me. Anyway, if she's only across the corridor you're more likely to get back together again—aren't you?'

'What's it all about, Bob?'

'I was going to ask you that. Whatever it is, I'd give her a while to calm down before you apologise and then start some serious grovelling.'

Apologise for what?'

'Does it matter—just do it. She's only just moved in and already I can't watch my own TV programmes—apparently she needs to catch up on her *Soaps*—it helps her grieving!'

'I'll come over later then?'

'Look Lee, leave it until tomorrow. I'll say you're really upset and wanted to come over but I told you to stay away. Things may be better after you've both had a night to think things over.'

'OK—but try and find out what I've done will you?'

'I'll do my best.' Lathom laughed, he looked at the list. 'First things first—can you find her hair straighteners?'

Once Lathom had left Melville sat on the sofa. Everything seemed so quiet and the apartment so bare; he'd forgotten how things used to be before Sheryl moved in. He switched on the TV then switched it off again and went and retrieved his diaries from under the bed. After meeting Isabella again after all these years he needed to revisit the past one more time. He sorted through the pile of books until he found a small leather-bound diary, its spine was embossed with the date: 1815.

§

1815

Melville was waiting with his regiment on the far side on Mont Sant Jean, the village of Waterloo a few hundred yards behind him. Wellington had placed most of his infantry on the reverse slope so that they were invisible to the French forces, a tactic he had used to good effect in Spain and Portugal during the Peninsula War. If your enemy has little idea of the strength of your forces or your disposition, then it makes them cautious and open to strategic errors. Until now Wellington had only faced Napoleon's generals in battle and, on several occasions, they'd been unnerved and ultimately undone by this tactic. Today was different; less than mile away across the valley Napoleon himself waited to launch the French assault on the British positions and, although Napoleon had suffered recent defeats, most notably in Russia a few years before, he was still acknowledged as a military genius with a reputation for surprising his enemies with his ability to react to the changing face of a battle instinctively and decisively. Although Melville and his troops felt relatively safe in their present position they knew only too well that they would soon be engaged in a brutal and bloody battle. About half of the troops under his command had fought before, the rest were raw recruits. They'd been well trained in the necessary tactics of an infantry regiment, but you could never be certain how they would react in the heat of battle. Discipline was all important; the troops who could stand and fight could triumph over a much superior force.

Napoleonic warfare was a particularly brutal version of paper, stone and scissors. The three main branches of the army had their individual strengths and weaknesses.

The infantry had three main formations:

Column: a dense mass of men marching together in a rectangle. This was the quickest way to move troops, but it was very vulnerable to artillery fire, and from musket fire from opposing infantry. However, it could easily defend itself against cavalry, even though it could only use a few of the muskets on the outside of the column.

Line: infantry spread out in a long line up to four men deep. This allowed them to bring all their muskets to bear on the enemy and, because they were spread out, made them less vulnerable to other infantry firing the inaccurate muskets of the period. It also made them relatively immune to artillery fire because the round shot tended to bounce between them. However, they were helpless against a cavalry charge, when the men would easily be scattered and cut down. Their muskets could only fire two or possibly three times a minute, and they were very inaccurate. The chance of shooting a rider on a moving horse was non-existent and once you'd fired your musket you would be cut down by a sabre or stabbed by a lance as you tried to run away.

Square: this was the infantry's defensive formation. The men formed a rough open square, four deep and approximately twenty-five men wide on each side. The first rank knelt with fixed bayonets, their musket's stock pushed into the earth to produce a fixed wall of steel. The second rank used their bayonets to stab at anyone attempting to break into the square. The third rank stood and fired their weapons, while the forth rank reloaded them and passed them to the third rank, enabling a rapid rate of fire. Due to the inherent inaccuracy of their muskets they were only effective if fired *en masse*. The infantry would reload, wait for the command to fire then all fire together. Squares were impenetrable for cavalry but a very soft target for artillery, and were vulnerable to infantry in line because they could only bring a very small proportion of their muskets to bear.

The difficultly for an infantry battalion was to try and keep in the correct formation at any particular time—or suffer enormous casualties. That was why discipline was so important: the soldiers needed to react to their officer's commands without a moment's hesitation. Poorly trained infantry would tend to panic and the formation would break down, resulting in annihilation for the whole battalion.

Melville looked at his men relaxing, laughing and joking, smoking and sitting or lying down on the hill side. They'd been instructed to keep out of sight until they were needed. They could hear the battle raging down in the valley but could only see the wounded being brought back loaded on wagons. These were the lucky ones, on their way to an appointment with the surgeons and their bone saws. Most of the wounded were left behind, maimed and left to die on the battlefield. If you were fortunate you would die quickly; the unfortunate could lie there in agony for hours or even days. After the battle scavengers would loot the dead and dying, cutting the throats of any who failed to give up their valuables. Bodies were stripped of their clothes and even their teeth were extracted to make dentures for the rich at home in Britain.

Melville had seen many of his friends killed and maimed in the years since he'd joined the army as a drummer boy. He was no stranger to the realities of war. He'd just returned from fighting the Americans in Canada with the 8th Foot and was due to start training new recruits to enable the regiment to replenish its strength after its losses in that campaign, but then Napoleon had escaped from Elba and the call had gone out from Wellington to raise a new army and he had volunteered. But why? Possibly out of some feeling of loyalty to Wellington; he would still be a corporal if it hadn't been for him. Or perhaps because he didn't know any other life than this—one battle after another, different faces, different countries, but always the familiar camaraderie of the regiment.

Today he felt different. He had something to live for other than glory; now he had Isabella. Their last meeting had been three days before when they'd cut their thumbs and let their blood mingle and pledged eternal love. He looked at his thumb which had begun to bleed slightly staining his white gloves and hoped this would the only blood he would shed today.

Then a rider approached with a dispatch from Wellington and twenty minutes later they were drawn up in column behind the ridge. The drum began a steady beat and Melville remembered playing the same beat himself years before and for a moment he was a frightened teenager once again. He quickly dismissed the memory and rallied his troops. They'd only walked a few hundred yards when the first artillery bombardment sliced through them, round shot bouncing up the hill towards them like a deadly bowling ball. The order was given to form a line and the battalion quickly dispersed, forming up four deep, muskets loaded and at the ready. But there was no enemy in range and they held their fire.

The battlefield was partially obscured by the smoke from the guns of both sides. He could only see a few hundred yards ahead of him and the noise of the artillery and musket volleys made it impossible to pass orders to his men. All communication was done by bugle or drum. Suddenly the bugle rang out and his blood ran cold.

'Prepare to receive cavalry—form a square!' he shouted.

No one could hear him, but they'd heard the bugle and immediately began to form a square. Their actions were automatic, the result of years of training. The experienced cajoled the novices and the square was hastily completed just as the first French cavalry galloped into view.

They were cuirassiers, the shock troops of the French cavalry. Each man was over six-foot tall, mounted on a heavy horse. They wore a burnished steel breast-plates and helmets with a long flowing crest of horse hair; each carried a short carbine and a long straight sword. They galloped flat out towards the square, their intention to panic the troops and make them scatter, but Melville's men were too experienced for that. They held their ground. He raised his sword above his head and let it fall at the last moment. The third rank of the square fired in unison and the forward rank of the French cavalry faltered under the force of the volley as their comrades fell, then they reined in their horses confronted by the wall of bayonets. They wheeled around and galloped off into the smoke. The inexperienced soldiers cheered but the others remained silent—this was no victory it had just begun.

They waited. The smoke began to clear, then Melville saw the cannons. This was the most difficult time for an infantry regiment. The artillery were too far away for a musket ball to reach them, but the infantry couldn't form a line because they knew the enemy cavalry were waiting out of sight for an opportunity to avenge their comrades.

All the infantry could do was stand and try to withstand the imminent bombardment.

Melville stood in the centre of the square facing the cannons. They were on a slope so he could see over the heads of his men. He had faced cannon like this twice before and he'd hoped never to do it again. The next few minutes would be critical. It all depended on discipline, if the square broke—they would all die.

Men had different ways of dealing with staring down the barrel of a cannon that would soon be killing and maiming you and your friends; some joked, some refused to look at the guns, a few thought they'd be able to dodge the balls at the last minute. Melville knew it made no difference. You just had to stand and take it; there was no alternative.

The first ball was aimed short. It hit the ground twenty yards in front of the square and bounced. The forward row of men ducked and it sailed over their heads, but smashed into the rear wall of the square where the men were facing away from the cannon and were taken unawares. Half a dozen men were smashed to pulp by it with broken limbs and skulls, the wounded screaming and clawing at the ground. There was no time to attend to them; the square had to be repaired before the cavalry returned.

'Close ranks!' Melville shouted above the mayhem.

The soldiers shuffled together, stepping over the wounded and dead, their feet slipping in the blood and gore. Melville had experienced this before and his ears were deaf to their screams. He looked to the cannon; he knew that they were just getting their range. Once they had it then they'd turn all the guns on the square and heaven help them.

The second cannon fired, this time a shell; it landed in front of the square. It was a rough ball like a cannon ball but it had a burning wick projecting from one side—the fuse. The men stared at it. It seemed to take forever, but it was only a few seconds; then it exploded scattering red hot shrapnel into the front ranks.

'Close ranks!'

The square was just closing up when the artillery commander decided that he had the correct range and fired his entire battery at the same time. It cut a huge swathe through the front rank. Melville tried to rally his men and close the breach, tried to pull the square into a triangular shape to close the void, but before this could be accomplished the cavalry returned.

The cuirassiers galloped up the hill and burst through the breach, swords swinging and bugles blowing. Melville's men were still holding their nerve and trying to close the breach with the horsemen inside—it was their only chance. The rear ranks turned inwards and shot at point-blank range. The outer ranks used their bayonets to try and fend off the remaining cavalry outside the square. The next few minutes would be critical.

Regiments imbued their flag or 'colour' with almost religious significance. To lose one's colour was the most humiliating thing that could happen to a regiment and the greatest prize for an enemy. A cuirassier tried to seize the regimental colour from the young ensign. The cavalry man slashed at the ensign and cut him down with one blow of his heavy sabre, he tried to pull the flag from the dying man but it was trapped under his body. The young drummer boy ran up and, seizing the ensign's halberd (a long pike with a spear at the top), he tried to fend off the cuirassier, an unequal struggle that must soon end in the boy's death. The cavalry man slashed wildly but the boy held his nerve and kept him at bay with the pike. Melville saw what was happening and ran to the boy's aid brandishing his sword and screaming to draw the cavalry man's attention. The cuirassier turned towards Melville, drew his short-barrelled carbine and fired at point-blank range. The musket ball hit Melville in the chest; he fell and was swallowed up the writhing mass of men and horses. He lay there, bodies clambering over him in the mayhem of war and felt the blood pouring from his wound, felt the strength ebbing from him with each ragged breath. He knew he was about to die, he sensed his consciousness slipping away. The cacophony of war was replaced by darkness and silence.

Two weeks later Melville was in a coach on the way back from a meeting with Isabella. The doctors had advised him against riding for a few more weeks. They still didn't understand how he'd survived the musket ball but, because it had been at such close range, the ball had passed straight through him and they'd had no need to operate. Now there was hardly a scar to show for it.

He'd been relieved to hear that the square had held and a company of British hussars had arrived just in time to chase away the remaining French cavalry and attack their cannon. The drummer boy had survived and at the end of the battle had come looking for Melville and found him trapped under a dead horse, but miraculously still alive. Now Melville felt stronger than he'd ever felt in his life—but also different, changed.

Isabella had explained the reason for this change, that she'd turned him into a vampire to save his life. He didn't believe her—she must be mad—but at least it proved she loved him. If she thought that sharing blood would make him immortal, then it proved that she wanted to live with him for ever—therefore their love must be true.

Why else would she want him to kill her husband?

Melville had never killed a man in cold blood, only in the heat of battle, and he considered her husband to be a friend. If she'd asked him to commit such a murder a few weeks ago he would have refused, but now it seemed the only option. He couldn't explain why this was so—perhaps he felt that he deserved some recompense for his suffering. After all, he'd risked his life and all those others had died to keep their country safe; why shouldn't a civilian make some sacrifice in return?

The following evening, he waited in an alley, a scarf tied around his face, a sharp knife in his hand. Isabella has assured him that her husband always took this route to his club and had made him promise to take her husband's purse so that it would look like a robbery that had gone wrong, then no suspicion would attach itself to either of them and they would be free to marry—and she would inherit her husband's money.

While he waited, Melville felt uneasy. Since the battle he'd had strange cravings and hallucinations, he felt he was losing his mind. Perhaps he was catching Isabella's madness and soon he'd think he was a vampire too. He tried to steady his nerve and focus his mind but all he could think about was blood. Perhaps that was due to his recent experiences at Waterloo? He'd seen more blood that day than he cared to remember. A memory of standing ankle deep in blood and entrails, the screams of the wounded and the whinnying of the dying horses, overcame him. He could feel sweat on his brow. He tried to clear his mind and calm himself.

Before he had time to compose himself Isabella's husband appeared in the alley. He was rushing along and looking down at his feet but, just as Melville was about to lunge at him with the knife, he looked up and recognised him, smiled and leaned forward to embrace him. Melville struck. Once, twice, three times he plunged the knife into Isabella's husband's chest and his victim fell to the floor, gasping and bleeding to death, he quickly searched him and took the small leather purse filled with coins.

As he put the purse in his coat pocket, Emma, Isabella's maid arrived. She was holding a pair of grey gloves and appeared to be trying to catch up with her master, who must have left them behind. When she saw her master on the floor mortally wounded and Melville searching him, she screamed. Melville knew there was no going back and struck again, he plunged the knife into her again and again.

He stood over the two bodies, appalled and disgusted by his actions. He knelt down and cradled the girl in his arms. She was young probably only in her early teens, no more than a child. He began to beg her forgiveness, tried to revive her, suddenly he saw the fresh blood and was overcome by a new and irresistible urge: he leaned over her and began to drink the blood as it pumped from her wound.

A short while later he was sitting in Isabella's parlour trying to explain what had happened. He wanted to go back and see if the girl was still alive but Isabella seemed indifferent to her fate. She told him not to worry, the girl had been lazy and it would be easy to find a replacement. Melville now realised what he'd done: he'd killed a friend and a child. Isabella appeared cold, not the passionate lover of a few weeks before. She appeared disappointed by Melville's reaction, and offered him the coins from her husband's purse. Melville was repulsed by the suggestion and left empty handed.

§

Melville closed the diary. Now Isabella had returned after two centuries, pledging her eternal love and claiming to have been misunderstood. Had he really been so mistaken all those years ago? Did she still love him? Did he still love her? Perhaps his diary held the truth? He opened it again and read further.

The following morning after a restless night he had made a decision: he'd go and see Sheryl and explain about Isabella, then they'd go and see Isabella together. They'd be all grown up about it, explain that he loved Sheryl and that Isabella meant nothing to him anymore, then they'd part amicably. Umm? Somehow he couldn't see that happening; vampires were notoriously territorial and that seemed to apply to people as well as places. And somehow he didn't like the idea of being in the middle of a tug of war. He knocked hesitantly at the door to 13F, which was opened by Bob looking harassed. Bob hadn't shaved and was wearing his dressing gown.

'Hi Lee, she's calmed down a bit. She's in the bath—come back in an hour.'

'Can't Bob, I've got an appointment, don't tell her I called—I'll explain everything later.'

Lathom shrugged. 'OK—if that's what you want.'

Melville called the lift and checked his watch; he'd go and see Isabella as arranged then come back and explain everything to Sheryl. If he managed to keep them apart he might still avoid a bloodbath.

A few hours later he was walking back towards the apartment after his meeting with Isabella, more confused than when he'd left. Could it be that Isabella still loved him and that he'd got things so wrong two hundred years before? He called the lift and it arrived with a 'ping', then pressed the 13th floor. Melville knew that he needed to talk to Sheryl immediately before things got completely out of hand. He tried to focus his mind, tried to make sense of the last twenty-four hours so that he could explain things to her clearly.

The floor indicator flashed:

10. Yesterday morning everything had made sense. Then Sheryl had suddenly stormed out and left him. But why? Did she think he was having an affair? He'd never done anything to make her think that was the case.

11. Then Isabella had reappeared after two hundred years and declared her undying love for him—when he'd always been convinced that she'd only thought of him as a means to an end. Perhaps he just didn't understand women?

12. After re-reading his diary last night he'd realised how much he'd loved Isabella and perhaps they'd only split up because he was having problems coming to terms with becoming a vampire. After all she'd only made him one in the first place so as to save his life.

13. The lift 'pinged'. Melville was deep in thought. The doors opened and Sheryl was facing him. Momentarily

taken aback, he tried to say something but they passed one another in the doorway and she refused to make eye contact with him.

'Look Sheryl we need to -,' he said.

Then the lift doors closed, cutting him off in mid-sentence and he watched the indicator above count down 12,.11.,10. He walked towards his apartment, changed his mind and knocked on Lathom's door. Half an hour later he was sitting on his own sofa trying to decide what to do next. His chat with Lathom hadn't really helped him understand what was going on and he still didn't know why Sheryl was so annoyed with him, nor if the sudden reappearance of Isabella was purely accidental or somehow linked. He sipped his coffee and stared at the silver parcel on the kitchen work surface; now he had Bob's bomb to dispose of as well. He checked his watch. He just had time to go and get some more flowers—if this carried on much longer he'd be on first names terms with the florist—then get a card, take them to Sheryl and explain about Isabella. After that he could go and see Isabella as arranged and try and make her understand that it was all over between them. He'd tried this morning, but it was as though she didn't want to believe it; she seemed to assume that Sheryl was just a friend and even asked him to bring her over this evening to meet her. Well, there was no way he was going to risk that until he was sure that they both understood the situation. He'd deserve more than a Victoria Cross if he was caught up in a dispute between vampires as to whose boyfriend he was.

Melville checked his watch again and put his mug in the sink. He'd take Lathom's advice, flowers first and a card; then apologise to Sheryl, even though he didn't know what he was apologising for; he'd even put on that new shirt that she'd bought him. He shuddered at the thought; he thought he looked like a contestant on *Strictly Come Dancing*—she loved it.

He returned from the shops with the gifts; a bouquet of red roses and a large card with a picture of a very sad puppy on the front. The woman in the card shop had assured him that it would be perfect for an apology, especially a non-specific one, and he still had no idea what he'd done. Was it something major or minor? He could never tell with women; perhaps he'd wiped one of the *Soaps* that she recorded? Perhaps he'd just left the top off the toothpaste again? The wording on the card needed to be contrite but vague—he'd didn't want to admit to something she didn't already know about—unfortunately he wasn't convinced by the result. His handwriting was spidery, neat but rather illegible. He'd learned to write with a quill but biros were a different matter entirely. The finished apology took the form of a short paragraph that was neat but indecipherable. It looked like a last will and testament written by a Victorian solicitor, not at all like the thoughts of a sad puppy. But he didn't have time to buy another card—it would have to do.

He changed into the shirt that Sheryl had bought him the previous week, which so far he'd managed to find excuses not to wear it in public. He looked in the mirror and was glad he had his sunglasses on; he found the weird geometric shapes and bright colours hurt his eyes. Well, at least there was one consolation, once it was on he didn't have to look at it himself. One of the advantages of being in the armed forces of whatever nation he had served in over the centuries had been that he never had to choose what to wear, which was an advantage as he was often confused as to what was considered fashionable at any particular time or place. Things seemed to change so quickly. Some time ago he'd adopted black as his unofficial civilian uniform and had stuck to it ever since. He stood in front of the bathroom mirror in the garish shirt, holding the flowers and rehearsing what he intended to say, which was apologetic in tone but also suitably vague. He'd rather be preparing to go into battle. He understood the rules of war; he really didn't understand women.

Melville knocked at Lathom's door and waited, knocked again and waited some more and then in desperation used the key that he had been given him to let himself in. The apartment was deserted, he must still be at the tug and therefore Melville had no idea where Sheryl was or when she would return. He was about to leave the flowers and card, then changed his mind. He really needed to talk to Sheryl if he was going to convince her that he hadn't done anything wrong; or if he had to find out what it was. He decided to call on Sheryl later on his way to meet Isabella at the Hilton; then he could see Isabella with a clean conscience and make sure that she understood that there was no future for them. Hopefully things would get back to normal and he could stop looking like a Spanish gigolo.

A few anxious hours later he was back. He knocked at the door to apartment 13F and it was opened by a bad tempered Lathom. Sheryl had gone out and he had no idea when she'd be back so Melville left the gifts after all, but then decided not to stay; he needed to explain to Sheryl about Isabella without her hearing anything second-hand from Lathom.

He'd just left the apartment building on his way to the Hilton when his phone rang. It was Isabella calling to cancel their meeting. They arranged to meet the following morning. Melville didn't complain because he was secretly relieved; with luck he'd be able to sort things out with Sheryl tonight. That would only leave a difficult meeting with Isabella in the morning for him to contend with.

Later that evening he was sitting in his apartment waiting; Lathom had agreed to contact him when Sheryl returned. Where was she? He switched on the app and saw Sheryl's symbol half-way up Seel Street. She must be in *their* bar; he decided to throw caution to the winds. He grabbed his coat and was about to leave the apartment when he saw that her symbol had begun to move slowly down Seel Street towards their apartment building. If he waited she'd soon be back at the apartments and she wouldn't need to know that he had set up a tracking app. He hung up his coat and decided to wait for her to get back. Suddenly the symbol stopped briefly and then, equally suddenly, moved off at speed. It must be a car, he thought; she was too close to need a taxi. Either she'd found herself a 'hot date' or she'd met up with someone she already knew from before they met. He still didn't know where she was living when they met—perhaps she'd met up with an ex-lover? He wasn't sure if he wanted to know what she was up to, switched off the app and went to bed.

Melville couldn't sleep; he had the feeling that he'd let his only real chance of happiness slip through his fingers. The longer he tried to keep Isabella's reappearance secret, the guiltier it made him seem. He tossed and turned. Why hadn't he told Sheryl immediately after he'd bumped into

Isabella outside the Hilton? He knew only too well—cowardice. He started to write a text message to try to explain, realised that it wouldn't do, that he would have to do it face to face. He deleted the text and sent her a short affectionate one instead. Once she was back home he could try to make her believe him; doing it by text would only make things worse.

A few hours later he was still awake. He sent another text apologising and asking her to call him back then, in desperation, he switched on the app—there was no sign of Sheryl's symbol. Either she had already returned to Lathom's apartment or she'd realised that he must be tracking her phone and switched it off. He couldn't wait any longer. He dressed and then knocked at 13F. Lathom opened the door almost immediately. Surprisingly considering the hour, he was dressed in his coat and hat.

'Hi Lee, come in—she's not back yet. I was just about to come and see you. I've made a decision.'

Melville walked into the lounge. There were piles of things on the sofa.

'Can you get rid of the weapons Lee? I've got what I need and it'll be difficult to explain the others when the police search the apartment.'

'Why would they do that?'

'Because I'm about to go missing.'

'Why?'

'That bomb could easily have killed Michelle or Natasha. The longer I stay here the more danger they're in. Once I disappear they'll be safe. I'm going to fake my own death so they'll inherit this apartment and my cottage, and then my ex-colleagues will stop looking for me.'

'What about you? Will you be OK, Bob?'

'I'll be fine—plenty of Kelly's money tucked away in my Swiss bank account. I'll just have to start again like you two do. I suppose I'll have to get used to that now I'm a vampire. By the way Lee—can you *sense* me yet?'

'No, not yet. It takes a while before you're properly one of *us*.'

'I don't really feel very different at the moment, perhaps when I can *sense* the others then I'll believe it's true.'

'What should I do with the bomb?'

'Throw it in the Mersey. It's completely safe unless you close the circuit.' Lathom buttoned up his coat.

'Why tonight?'

'They've got impatient Lee, decided to spring the trap. Just had a call from an old friend who needs to talk to me urgently—it won't wait.'

'What are you going to do?'

'Go. They'll expect the bomb to go off—they won't expect me to turn up.'

'Why go at all?'

'I want to see my friend—find out why he called me.'

'What then?'

'Sorry Lee, best not to tell anyone.' Lathom picked up his car keys. 'Give my regards to Sheryl and look after Natasha and Michelle for me. Hope we meet again sometime.' He held out his hand.

'Bound to Bob, sometime.'

They shook hands; then Lathom was gone.

Melville sat on the sofa looking at the flowers and the unopened card on the table. He bundled the weapons into Sheryl's old backpack and picked up the hockey stick case.

He decided to put them and the bomb in his car now rather than clutter up his apartment. He could take them to Sheryl's storage locker tomorrow. Melville checked his phone again; still no sign—where was she?

CHEAPSIDE

Peter was trying to concentrate on his trial but his mind was on something else. What was the matter with Natasha? Was it post-traumatic stress like her doctor had said or something else? Ever since she'd been abducted she'd been distant and constantly preoccupied. Often he'd be talking to her and realise that she wasn't listening, that her mind was on something else—something she wouldn't discuss. He'd tried to talk about it but she'd just cut him short and change the subject.

She'd agreed to see the therapist after she started seeing her dead nan. It only ever happened when she was alone, that's what she'd told him, but he wasn't sure that was the truth. Once or twice he'd caught her staring at the armchair in her mum's flat that had been her nan's as though watching someone. When he'd spoken to her it was as though she'd been snapped out of a trance.

They said it was grief and that the hallucinations would soon stop but he wasn't so sure. The doctors had signed her off for a month and the hospital had been very supportive. Some of her colleagues had been over to see her but she was just as distant with them. She'd spend all day sitting in her mum's flat in silence while her mum was working; she didn't even watch the TV. It was decided that she should get out more and she'd started going with her mum to help her at the apartments. They thought that mixing with her mum's clients would help her regain her confidence and also that she needed a hobby.

Natasha had always been good on the computer and one of her friends from the ward suggested researching her family history. It seemed to help and she started drawing up the Malone family tree. It was surprising how many of them there were: every generation seemed to have a half a dozen children with even more cousins and second cousins. 'Well we've always been a 'good Catholic family,' explained Michelle with a smile when Peter had commented on it.

Peter's family by comparison was Protestant and their family tree was suitably stunted. Natasha had decided to do his family while she was waiting for some copies of birth certificates from Ireland to arrive for hers'. Within two days she'd managed to trace his family back to the middle of the nineteenth century, when Cornish miners had come north looking for work. The family had settled in Liverpool and then become shopkeepers. Peter looked at the family tree with interest. His great, great, great grandfather had been Charles, one of three brothers, and had served in the First World War; two of them had survived the War, the other one had died in the trenches. Peter felt rather inadequate because his family tree didn't quite fill a sheet of A4 whereas Natasha's covered an entire dining-room table, a huge spidery web of Saint's names and dates.

Peter checked his watch his heart wasn't really in it today. He decided to have an early lunch hoping that he'd feel more focused that afternoon. He cleared away his notes and took his sandwich box from his backpack under the desk. The food in the student cafeteria seemed to be getting even worse of late and for the past few weeks he'd been bringing a packed lunch. Usually he ate it at his desk but because today was sunny, he decided to go for a walk instead.

A few minutes later he was in Abercromby Square and enjoying one of Natasha's 'experimental' sandwiches. Today's appeared to be tuna with beetroot and rocket, which he considered a resounding success compared to some of the others. He finished his lunch and stretched out in the sun. The square was quite quiet at the moment as it was still half an hour until the morning lectures finished, Peter tried to clear his mind and concentrate on his trial.

As far as he could tell he had actual created immortal mice and he'd proved that by giving them certain blood products he could maintain their health. Unfortunately this seemed to do little for their temperament and they were still very aggressive. Unless he could sort that out there was no way the authorities would give approval for primate trials; no one wanted a lab full of psychotic chimps with blood lust.

In fact, he'd had an experience the other morning that had rather shaken him up and brought home to him the enormity of what he was embarking upon. Early DNA tests on the sample mice had confirmed stabilisation of their telomeres. However, to gauge the effect on their organs he needed tissue samples and had decided to euthanase one of the trial mice so that he could have the organs analysed. Analysis would, he hoped, confirm that the blood products had fully controlled the vitamin deficiencies he'd detected earlier.

There was a set protocol for the euthanasia of laboratory mice. The mouse was placed in a sealed chamber which allowed it room to run around. The chamber had a separate air supply and gradually the oxygen concentration was reduced and the level of carbon dioxide increased, this was done over a long period of time so as not to stress the animals. Slowly but surely they would become drowsy and eventually unconscious. Once unconscious the oxygen was turned off and they were exposed to 100% CO_2 for a few minutes, at the end of which they were dead. Peter was always overcautious as far as this was concerned and on this occasion he'd left the mouse exposed to CO_2 for much longer than most of his colleagues would usually do.

When eventually he turned off the CO_2 and removed the mouse, it was already cold to the touch, he laid it out on the dissection board and pinned its limbs with long steel needles pushed hard into the wood. Then he took a scalpel and made an incision to open up the abdomen so that he could harvest the organs for analysis.

He was about to remove the mouse's liver when—it woke up. He was so surprised that he dropped the scalpel on the floor. Rather than appearing traumatised or distressed the mouse appeared to be angry. It started flexing its body and arching its back, attempting to get free. When it tore one of its hind legs free, Peter snapped out of his trance. He grabbed the scalpel from the floor and severed its spinal cord. Then for good measure he decapitated it and placing the severed head on the table alongside its body while he proceeded to remove the organs; He was badly shaken, and its beady eyes seemed to watch him with contempt as he worked.

He'd sent the organs for analysis and had received the results that morning. It appeared that the blood products he'd given the mice had indeed corrected the vitamin deficiencies. In future he'd be able to give them supplements in their diet rather than have to give them fresh blood as he'd first envisaged. Unfortunately, he was still no closer to finding a way of modifying their behaviour. Could it be that immortality and aggression were inextricably linked? If that was the case, then he'd never get approval for the primate trials. He shuddered as he remembered the strength of the mouse that had torn its own foot free from the steel pin; its fury and its disregard for physical pain. Imagine, what a chimp would be capable of—or a man? He would need to take things very carefully from now on. He couldn't risk announcing his findings until he was sure that he could control the side effects.

'Remember Frankenstein, Pete,' he said to himself, 'He only wanted to do good—look what happened to him.'

That afternoon he left the lab early. He'd written up his interim findings and couldn't do any more until he received the last of the test results from toxicology tomorrow. He took the opportunity to drive over to the retail park and pick up some more decorating materials. His tenants had finally moved out of his old apartment in Cheapside, the one he had shared with Rachel prior to her death. Natasha was planning to move in with him soon because her mum was due to move back to her old flat off London Road in a few weeks. While he was living alone it would be an ideal opportunity to re-decorate, he decided. His friend Ben had agreed to come over that evening and help him emulsion the living room walls with the promise of beers and a pizza to follow.

Later that evening, they were sitting around the kitchen table, which was covered in a dust sheet. A pile of empty take-away boxes were stacked by the pedal bin and Peter had just opened two more beers.

'Thanks for helping, Ben—I do appreciate it.'

'No worries Pete, I enjoyed it. How are things with Tash?'

'So-so, she's got a new counsellor—fingers crossed.'

'Give her my best. What about your psycho mice?'

'Vampire mice.'

'Whatever—is there a difference?'

'Yes, it's all to do with metabolism not psychoses.'

'No, I mean; if they're still violent little bastards—does it matter why?'

'It does if you want to control the aggression and move on to the primate trials.'

'Will they let you do that?'

'Perhaps. There's just one problem: I don't know if I'm going to do it. I don't even know if I'm going to carry on with the project.'

'Why not? What about your job and the PhD?'

'What if I let vampire chimps loose on the world? Or worse—vampire *men*?'

'*Men?*'

'Imagine what certain governments could do with this research. What could North Korea for example do with an army of immortal soldiers with blood lust and no fear?'

'See what you mean. But you will be able to control it—won't you?'

'Perhaps, perhaps not. It doesn't matter though. Once I publish, any lab in the world can make its own vampire mice, and then all anyone has to do is inoculate something or someone with the blood from one of those mice. You wouldn't even know vampire men were among us—no pointy teeth or capes to give them away. And if my mice are anything to go by they wouldn't change into bats or be affected by sunlight.'

'Are you sure about this, Pete?'

'Not positive, but close enough to be worried. Put it this way, Ben—I'm very careful when I handle the mice. I use heavy gloves and eye protection. There's no way I'm going to be the first primate trial.'

'At least I know you're not one already.'

'How?'

'Well, you've just eaten garlic bread.'

They both laughed.

§

Natasha didn't know why she was here, she must be mad to return to a place where she'd so nearly died. Perhaps she was mad; after all she'd been having weird dreams and hallucinations during the day. He therapist had said that it was all post-traumatic stress coupled with grieving for her nan. She toyed with the key in her pocket and its heavy key ring. Why had she taken it from Sheryl's apartment in the first place? She'd have to remember to borrow her mum's key to their apartment tomorrow and put it back before they noticed it was missing.

As she passed through the arch into the cobbled courtyard of Rumford Court, the memories came flooding back. Her abduction at Festival Park and that terrifying night bound and blindfolded at the mercy of a psychopath, her mind full of strange images brought on by the drugs he'd given her. She still didn't know if the dreams were fact or fiction.

What had happened between Kelly and Sheryl? What was all that bit about the Lone Ranger and Tonto? It was obvious that they'd met before and Lee was somehow involved too. But what did that have to do with the shootings at the apartment and Bob? How come he'd suddenly appeared on the scene and was conveniently her long lost granddad? Then, on top of that, Peter was convinced he'd created vampire mice. Perhaps she was the only sane one and everyone else was mad?

She crossed the courtyard and remembered Sheryl dragging her away from Kelly and him driving off in his 4X4. She remembered that he'd seemed amused by it all, even when Sheryl seemed about to shoot him. What had he said as he was about to leave? 'See you around sucker'. Did he mean that? Would he come back? She shuddered at the thought.

The key turned easily in the lock, but as she pushed the door a pile of junk-mail on the mat stopped it opening fully. Suddenly she panicked. Had Kelly already come back? She knew that the police didn't know his name or where he lived so they wouldn't be looking for him here. Sheryl had told her exactly what to tell the police; a selected version of the truth, neglecting to include this address. As far as they were concerned it was a robbery that had gone wrong. She'd been abducted that morning from reception and not the night before and had been held in the back of the 4X4 while they raided the apartments. Bob had surprised the robbers and they'd shot him and one of the thieves had been shot by someone else or by his associates by accident. According to the story, she'd been drugged and then dumped on the Strand when the robbers fled the scene—where she'd been found by Sheryl and Lee who were returning from a trip on the Mersey ferry.

Natasha thought it all sounded too far-fetched for anyone to believe but, surprisingly, the police seemed to accept it and the case had been dropped. Sheryl had said something about Bob having friends in high places and that the 'robbery' was to do with something 'hush-hush' from years ago when he was some sort of *'James Bond'*. Granddad Bob—James Bond? Now that was mad.

She pushed again and the door opened; closed it behind her and bolted it; she didn't want to be interrupted—especially by Kelly. The flat was just as she remembered it from her nightmares but strangely she felt calm now that she was there. She checked each room. Everything appeared to be exactly as when she was last here with Sheryl. Once Kelly had driven off they'd come inside while they waited for Lee to arrive and Sheryl had run through exactly what she wanted Natasha to tell the police. Natasha had been disorientated by the effect of the drugs Kelly had given her and by the events of the last twenty-four hours and had said little in reply.

Natasha walked into the main room and sat on arm of the sofa. This was where she'd sat while they waited for him. She saw the bullet hole in the top of the desk

So it wasn't a dream; it really had happened. Her attention was caught by something on the floor under the desk, she knelt down and picked it up. It was a cut-throat razor. She opened it and studied the blade, which had an inscription that she couldn't read properly because it was covered in something. She licked her finger and rubbed it off. 'Kelly's Matchless' it read. She sniffed her fingers and felt a sudden compulsion to taste it. She put her fingers to her lips; it tasted metallic, then she realised—it was blood. This must be Kelly's razor and have fallen out of his coat when Sheryl searched his pockets and found the other gun. She closed the razor and put it in her pocket. She needed to search the flat thoroughly in case there was anything else hidden away that might enable her to explain all that had happened.

She started in the bedroom. It was furnished in an opulent style like something from Sleeping Beauty's castle, but her memories were more nightmare than fairy-tale. She looked at the large gilded four-poster bed and shuddered. What had happened between her and Kelly? She could remember him touching her and she suddenly felt nauseous. Her memories were confusing and distorted by fear and the drugs he'd given her. Perhaps he hadn't done anything other than grope her, or perhaps she'd blotted it out? She knew from her nursing course that people often blot out memories that are too painful for them to deal with. That was part of post-traumatic stress syndrome. But what if? How would Peter react? No—that thought was too dangerous. She'd deal with that if and when—not now. She shut the door to the bedroom and moved on to the bathroom.

A search of the rest of the flat provided nothing of any significance. The only thing left was the computer and the first image that appeared when she switched it on was the screen saver—a graphic sexual image of a child. She swore and was about to switch it off, then realised that

that was his intention—shock tactics to stop anyone prying further. She'd done a course on child abuse and had also spent time working in theatre. When you first started your training you empathised too much, looked at the patient on the table and felt their pain, their anguish. Then you learned to put up a barrier to stop it damaging you, to let you do your job. Natasha decided to treat Kelly's picture gallery as she would a particularly gruesome road-traffic accident—with professional detachment.

Once through the first few grotesque images she managed to get into his files. The person who had used this computer, she assumed it was Kelly, obviously had limited computer skills. Very little was protected by passwords and those files that were she managed to hack into quite easily. She'd been pretty good at IT at school and it only took a few minutes to download a program to help her hack into the more difficult files. Most were bank statements from accounts all over the world and all had large amounts of money in them, except one 'Oreto Holdings' that had nothing in it. She couldn't transfer any of the money even if she wanted to because she'd need access codes for that and they were too well protected for her simple hacking programme.

Then she found a strange folder labelled '*Soft centres*'. She opened the file which appeared to be a list of names and dates in different colours, hundreds and hundreds of them, going back to the nineteenth century. It was laid out like a spread sheet, each entry started with a place and a date, then 'm' or 'f'—she assumed that was male or female—then an age followed by a surname and then first name. She scrolled back to the beginning, the first entry read:

'Liverpool 21/3/1862—m—26—Kelly—Stephen Patrick.'

Was it just a record of people and places? Who was this man Stephen Patrick Kelly who lived in Liverpool in 1862? How was he related to that sick paedophile, Kelly?

Natasha looked at the top of the spreadsheet and saw that it could be reorganised using surnames rather than in chronological order. She re-set it to list entries in alphabetical order and the file rearranged itself—but the different colours remained. The entries were in red, blue or green. Nearly every entry was green, with a few red and even fewer blue. Perhaps the surnames would help explain how Kelly was connected to the others.

She entered 'Melville' and then 'Lathom', but neither were listed. Then, she decided to see if she was listed so she entered 'Malone'. There were three entries; two in green, one blue. The first green one read:

'Malone—Shirley Bernadette—f—21—Liverpool 19/9/1962.'

This was strange. Natasha had a great aunt called Shirley but she was in Australia. How could she be connected to Kelly?

The second green one read:

'Malone—Jean Frances—f—62—Liverpool 11/5/15.'

Why did he have a record of her nan and the date of her death? The last entry was even more disturbing, it was in blue and read:

'Malone—Natasha Jean—f—22—'

However instead of a place and a date it said simply *'Pending'*.

She shivered and quickly clicked back onto the main page and scrolled through the names. What was the significance of the colours? Given Kelly's character she guessed that blue meant alive—at least for the time being—but then green couldn't mean dead assuming that the Shirley Bernadette Malone was her great aunt in Australia—they got a Christmas card ever year. And what about the red ones? She had to scroll through a lot of names before she found a red one:

'Flanagan—William—m—29—Liverpool—27/10/1974.'

What was the significance of William Flanagan? Why was he in red? There was final column which was usually blank, but for Flanagan's entry it read:

'See; O'Neil—William.'

She typed O'Neil. The entry in green read:

'O'Neil—William—m—29—Liverpool—28/3/1862.'

Other than Liverpool, their age and their first name, how were these two men connected? If anything she was even more confused than when she'd started. She took a receipt from her purse to note down the names and dates then found that her pen had run out of ink. She searched Kelly's desk to find another and in the bottom drawer found a small tobacco tin. It contained a random selection of items which she emptied it onto the desk: three different buttons, a small silver brooch, a wristwatch and a cloth label from IKEA, giving cleaning instructions and a name, *VORK*. There was no pen. She replaced the items; she'd have to try and remember some of the dates—or risk returning again. Perhaps once she'd had time to think it through she'd be able to make sense of it all.

§

Peter was still unsure what to do about his research but decided that if all else failed he would need a safety net. To this end he'd started a small parallel trial to see if he could 'cure' his vampire mice. His professor had allocated him extra funds to continue the original trial and he'd used some of this money to develop another retro virus that would re-activate a mouse's telomeres. He hoped that if this worked they would lose their immortality and hopefully their aggression as well.

Before using the retro virus on one of his vampire mice, he decided to try it on a normal mouse. Since a normal mouse had normally functioning telomeres the new retro virus should have no effect, he assumed, however once he'd inoculated it the mouse had immediately become lethargic and died within a few days. He'd had its tissues analysed hoping to find out what had killed it and was surprised to learn that it had died of old age. It appeared that by re-activating the telomeres of a normal mouse he'd somehow triggered a form of progenia, the genetic abnormality in humans that causes children to age quickly and die young, the condition that his original trial had been designed to cure.

This left him in a quandary: if he tried to 'cure' someone who he suspected might have been infected by his vampire mice, he could just as easily kill them as cure them. Consequently, he would need to be certain that they really were 'vampires' before he could use his 'cure' on them.

§

Natasha had offered once again to help her mum with the cleaning at the apartments but Michelle had tried to refuse because she preferred to work alone. It always seemed to take twice as long when Natasha came with her. Natasha had been insistent and, because everyone seemed to believe that it was helping her recovery, Michelle relented.

By mid-morning they were in an apartment on the 14th floor. Natasha never did much cleaning anyway. The real reason she'd been so keen to come was to try to return Kelly's key to Sheryl's apartment. She'd had a duplicate key cut the day before so that she could return to Kelly's apartment at will and all she needed to do now was return the original key to 13C before anyone noticed that it was missing—but she needed an excuse to visit the apartment. Her mum was cleaning the lounge and Natasha was sitting on a chair trying to talk to her above the noise of the hoover. She'd brought her family tree and was intending to visit the Central Library after returning the key and was idly playing with her earring and looking through her notes when an idea came to her. While Michelle was preoccupied Natasha carefully removed one of her earrings and tucked it in her pocket.

'Mum, I lost an earring the other day. You haven't seen it have you?'

'Wot's it like?'

'One of these.' She flicked the remaining earring with her finger. 'Those silver dangly ones Pete bought me.'

'I thought yer 'ad them in this mornin'?'

'No, just the one. It's a pity—they were the first thing he ever bought me. You don't think they could be in one of the apartments we cleaned the other day?'

'*We*' thought Michelle. As far as she could remember she'd been the only one doing any cleaning. 'Dunno—go an' knock an' ask if yer like.'

'What if they're out—couldn't I borrow your keys?'

'Suppose so, ther' on the side by me bag.'

Natasha took the keys. 'Won't be long. Then we can finish off in here.'

Michelle muttered something that was drowned out by the sound of the hoover.

Natasha took the back stairs down one floor, it was quicker than waiting for a lift. She knocked at Sheryl's apartment and waited, then knocked again. She opened the door with the key and quickly replaced Kelly's key in the drawer and had just closed the door when the lift opened and Sheryl got out. Reacting quickly, she knocked on the door again apparently unaware that Sheryl was behind her.

'Hiya hun, you looking for me?'

'Oh, Hi Sheryl, sorry to be a pain but I've lost an earring—I wondered if you'd found one? I was helping me mum with the cleaning the other day when it went missing. I wouldn't usually bother but its got sentimental value.'

Sheryl unlocked the door. 'Come on in; I haven't seen it but it's worth a look.'

Natasha made a half-hearted attempt at searching the carpet. Then slipped the earring out of her pocket while Sheryl's back was turned, then stood up and held it out in front of her and exclaimed: 'Found it!'

'Tea or coffee?'

'Well I should be getting back, give me mum a hand.'

'Go on keep me company.'

'OK, coffee—white, no sugar.'

They sat at the table chatting when Sheryl noticed the folder. 'Doing some studying?'

'No, it's genealogy. I'm tracing the Malone family tree.'

'I love things like that, let's have a look.'

Natasha spread the papers out on the table.

'Looks dead complicated. How far back have you got?'

'1830's so far.'

'Is this your mum?'

'Yeah,' Natasha pointed to another line, '—and that's me nan and her cousin Bobby.'

'The one who married Winnie from Jamaica?'

'Yes, how did you know that? I haven't written her in yet.'

'Oh, haven't you?' Sheryl looked again at the chart. 'Must have been something your nan said to me. Wasn't she the black one?'

Natasha nodded. 'Yes, perhaps that's why you remembered it?'

Sheryl decided to change the subject.

'Who's the first then?'

'Anne Mary Donnelly, born 1834 in Dublin, came over during the potato famine, died here when she was still in her twenties.'

'That's young to die, even then.'

'She was murdered.'

'Murdered?'

'In a churchyard. I've even found a newspaper clipping about it.'

'What happened then? Where did all this lot come from?'

'She had a daughter Mary who was eight and she went into an orphanage, married a John Patrick Malone when she was eighteen. I don't know where he came from yet, I'm waiting for some more records from Ireland to come through.'

Sheryl looked at all the names on the sheet. 'And all these came from those two?'

Natasha laughed. 'Well, me mum says we've always been a good catholic family.'

Sheryl smiled. 'Well, they didn't have the telly did they? I suppose you'll be the next one adding to the list?'

'Sorry?'

'You and Pete—you know? Patter of tiny feet?'

'Oh, I don't know about that.' Natasha was suddenly subdued and Sheryl sensed something was wrong.

'What's the matter hun? You and Pete had a domestic?'

'No, nothing like that … It's just been difficult since *it* happened. I don't know if I'm going mad; I see strange things all the time.'

Sheryl suddenly felt anxious and put her hand on Natasha's arm. 'What sort of things?' she asked.

'Dead people, I see me nan all the time … and she talks to me.'

'What else?'

Natasha started to cry.

'I feel so angry sometimes,' she sniffed, 'as though I could kill someone. I've started to crave strange things.'

'What things?'

Natasha shook her head and continued to sob. 'Can't—won't.'

Sheryl squeezed her arm. 'Look you can tell me anything; I won't be shocked, honest. It only natural that you're shook up by what happened.'

'But … what did happen? All I know for sure is that *he* kidnapped me and gave me drugs, and you rescued me, but no one has explained how or why. Even the police weren't interested; it's as though it never happened, as though it was all a dream. Perhaps it was. You told me it was all to do with

Bob's—I mean Granddad's past in Northern Ireland but Kelly said something to you about family—about the Lone Ranger and Tonto. What did that mean? It's so confusing; I don't know what was true and what was due to the drugs.'

'You were confused and frightened.' Sheryl smiled and squeezed her arm again. 'The mind can play tricks. Don't worry you're safe now—we'll make sure of that.'

'We? Who are *we*?'

'Can't say babe, it's hush-hush. The main thing is, Kelly isn't coming back—ever.'

'But what if he did *something* to me?'

'What did he do? Did he make you bleed?'

'No—but what if he raped me? What if he made me pregnant –what would Peter do? I can't remember anything clearly. My therapist thinks I may be blocking it out but I'm not sure. I think I was so out of it on the drugs that anything could have happened and I wouldn't know.'

'He wouldn't have done anything while you were drugged, a sick bastard like him wants you to be aware of what he's doing. Don't worry babe there's no chance that you're pregnant.'

Natasha sniffed and wiped away a tear. 'You sure about that?'

'Deffo babe, trust your aunty Sheryl.'

'Aunty?'

'Just a turn of phrase luv.' Sheryl let go of Natasha's arm and stood up, 'Somehow, ever since your nan thought I was her sister, you and your mum have felt like family to me.'

'What about your real family?'

'All dead long ago—fancy another coffee?'

§

Peter had had another sleepless night, haunted by images of a vampire army. He knew what he had to do. He had no intention of being responsible for the collapse of civilisation; no PhD was worth that risk. He needed to falsify his results to make it appear that his research had failed. However, just in case he ever managed to work out how to cure Progenia without the unpleasant vampire side effects, he'd need to keep the original results as well.

It was early Saturday morning and Natasha was still sleeping. He slipped out of bed and left a note by the kettle to say that he was going to the lab for a few hours. The lab would be empty on a Saturday, giving him free access to the computers; he could alter his results and make a copy of the originals without anyone being aware of it. All he needed was something to store the data—his laptop was too public. He rummaged in the kitchen drawer, he'd seen something suitable there the other day when he was looking for some batteries. Natasha had bought it for him last week as a joke. At the time he hadn't been amused and had thrown it in the drawer in disgust but now it was perfect. It was a memory stick in the shape of *Mickey Mouse*.

Natasha woke to find the note from Peter. He was often at the lab over the weekends so she thought no more about it. She knew that he was having problems with his research at the moment, but he'd stopped discussing it and, since she secretly found it boring, she'd been grateful not to have to pretend to be interested. She made some coffee and checked the post that lay on the mat but it was all for the old tenants. She hadn't officially moved into Peter's flat yet; it was still being redecorated and most of the furniture was in storage or under dustsheets.

She'd only stayed here last night because they'd gone clubbing with Ben and Helen and they'd decided to crash-out here rather than get a taxi to her mum's flat and disturb her in the early hours of the morning. She took a dust sheet off the coffee table, put her cup down and found Peter's laptop. She was bored and as they hadn't bought a TV yet, she decided to do some 'window shopping' on-line to pass the time.

She switched on the laptop and entered his password; she'd used her program to find that out ages ago. She didn't think of it as an invasion of privacy; it was more like a safety net. Her last boyfriend had cheated on her and her dad had cheated on her mum before he dumped her so there was no harm in occasionally having a browse through Peter's emails. So far he'd passed the test with flying colours, in fact she'd been slightly disappointed to find how squeaky clean he was. There were no dodgy emails or porn. It was all either work or things to do with Sci-Fi. Her first impressions of him had been true; he was a nerd—but a lovable one. She smiled as she looked through his *e-bay* account, then frowned when she saw how much he'd really paid for that plastic light-sabre that he'd told her had cost £15. Could an obsession with the Jedi Knights be grounds for divorce? She smiled; one thing she was sure of is that they'd have to get married first. Then another thought came into her head and her mood changed: her dad had left her mum when he found out that she was pregnant; her Nan's boyfriend had left her when he realised that her mum, Michelle wasn't his child; how would Peter react if she was pregnant and if the child might be Kelly's?

She decided that a little retail therapy at Peter's expense would improve her mood. If he could spend that much on a toy then they could definitely afford that table lamp she'd seen in IKEA the other week. Then she remembered the cloth tag from Kelly's apartment. She was still on *e-bay* so she entered '*IKEA VORK*'—an image appeared that surprised and confused her. There were two for sale but she wouldn't be buying one—they already had one.

She thought back to the items in Kelly's tobacco tin. Perhaps they were souvenirs—but of what? She had already decided that she'd have to visit his apartment again because she needed to check the dates and names on his spread sheet. Now that she had a duplicate key, all she needed was a way to store the data. She heard a key turning in the front door, quickly closed the laptop and covered it with the dustsheet. Peter came in carrying a can of paint.

'Hi Tash, picked up some more gloss while I was out. Thought I'd get a bit more done this afternoon.'

'Hiya Pete,' she put her mug on the work surface trying to disguise the fact that she'd been sitting by his laptop. 'How are the psycho mice this morning? Have they grown fangs yet or do they still look like my old mouse Derek?'

Peter was puzzled. 'How do you know what they look like?'

'I saw them—when we went to your lab that day, remember?'

'But you didn't go in the 'Animal Room'.'

'Yes I did—looking for you.'

'Did you handle them?'

'Not likely, vicious little buggers—tried to take a bite out of me.'

'Did they bite you? This is important Tash –did they?'

'No—I'd have said.' She remembered the scratch but decided not to mention it, 'Why?'

'You need to be careful with those mice; you could catch something.'

Natasha laughed, 'Well if I start craving cheese and grow big ears I'll blame it on you.'

He stared hard at her, smiled and decided not to probe any further—it would only end in an argument. She'd been quite aggressive lately and very easily provoked. The therapist had told him it was due to post-traumatic stress and to try and be more understanding. He'd be glad when she was back to normal, all this pent up anger and talking to her dead nan wasn't natural. He switched on the kettle and while her back was turned took the opportunity to put the memory stick back in the kitchen drawer. That was his proof that his trial had actually worked. Once he'd found another way to stabilise the telomeres without the unfortunate side effects, he'd be able to use the data again. Until that time he had to keep it safe and there was only the one copy. All the files at work had now been deleted and he didn't want to risk dropping the memory stick in the paint while he was decorating that afternoon.

They spent the rest of the day carefully painting the skirting boards with gloss paint. Natasha seemed her old self and Peter was sure that things would get easier once they moved in together. Michelle was always friendly when he stayed over but he always felt that he was in the way, found it difficult to be relaxed and never felt at home. Now he and Natasha would have their own home—although he still harboured reservations about returning to the apartment that he and Rachel had lived in prior to her death. After Rachel's fall, he'd felt responsible but once he'd had that strange angel dream all that had passed. Now he just felt sad for a lost life, two lives if you counted their unborn baby. He began to calculate how old the child would have been if they'd lived but quickly tried to put it from his mind. He shouldn't live in the past; he had a new future with Natasha—perhaps in time they'd have a child too? He'd even tried to discuss his misgiving with Natasha, but she'd appeared unconcerned, only insisting that they re-decorate and that she got to choose the colours and any new soft furnishings. He'd agreed immediately; he hated anything to do with interior design. He looked at his can of paint and smiled, only an interior designer would call this colour 'Sahara Sunrise'. He was a scientist; as far as he was concerned, it was beige.

Natasha watched Peter as he painted, and smiled, he looked so cute the way he stuck out his tongue when he was concentrating, that and the way his collar always stuck up on one side. She should be feeling happy—this was to be their first home together—however she still felt uneasy. This was the first serious relationship she'd had other than her 'ex' who'd cheated on her with a friend. The Malone women never seemed to have stable relationships with men; her mum had been dumped by her dad, Tom Richardson when she became pregnant, and her Nan had split up with her boyfriend after her mum had been born. Even her Great aunt Shirley in Australia was alone. What was it with men, was it because they never grew up and couldn't cope with the responsibility? She looked at Peter again. His tongue was stuck out and as he knelt to paint the door frame his unruly hair made him look like an overgrown school boy playing with his toys. What would he do it she was pregnant—run away?

She chased the thought from her mind and carried on with her painting and another thought came into her head: she needed some way to copy Kelly's files next time she visited his apartment. The few details she remembered from last time had raised more questions: who were all these people and how were they linked? It was like one of her family trees but they didn't seem to be related to one another. But there must be some connection. If she had all the names no doubt she could work it out. All she needed was a way to transfer the data; she could email it to herself, but that would leave a trail. What if the police searched Kelly's apartment and found his paedophilic gallery? She didn't want to be connected to that. Then she thought of something that she'd spotted the other day when she was looking for some *sellotape*: the *Mickey Mouse* memory stick she'd bought for Peter as a joke. He wouldn't miss it, after all he'd thrown it in the drawer and forgotten about it. It would be prefect.

Peter tried to concentrating on his painting, but his mind was on other things. He not only had to destroy the data of his trial but also the mice. It'd be no use protesting that the trial had failed if he had an animal room full of immortal psycho mice. Luckily he now had a way to dispose of them without anyone suspecting; all he had to do was inoculate them with his new retro virus and that would destabilise their telomeres and any subsequent analysis would show them to be normal mice once again. He'd have to do it when the lab was empty. If he'd thought, he could have done it this morning and then the mice would be showing signs of deteriorating health by early next week, and if he left it too long there was just the chance that the professor would ask to see his data and there was no time to fabricate a new set of results. He realised that his chance of a PhD was much less certain with a failed trial but there was no way he would risk being responsible for the collapse of civilisation for a permanent staff job and a parking space. Peter decided to visit the lab that evening; inoculate the mice, then write up the fake results, all he needed was some time to himself. He suggested to Natasha that it was probably best for her not to sleep at the apartment due to the paint fumes affecting her asthma. He was expecting an argument and was surprised when she readily agreed. It was a mild evening and the apartment was on the 12th floor so it'd be safe to leave the balcony windows open for the fumes to escape while he was at the lab. Peter felt much more relaxed. By tomorrow he'd have finished the decorating, inoculated the mice and re-written his notes.

There was no hurry. He wouldn't be able to visit the lab until the cleaners had left. If the department suspected foul play they might ask for his laptop and have it analysed to look for any deleted or amended files. The Jim Carver affair with the bald chimps a few years ago had been such a disaster that they were very mindful of the possibility of dishonest researchers making their results seem more impressive than they really were. There was also the opposite possibility: of researchers making their results appear less impressive while selling the real data to a private company—for a genuine breakthrough the financial rewards could be enormous. How much would the gift of immortality be worth? Probably more money than Peter could ever spend. No, he would remain poor—but guilt free. Perhaps he'd eventually work out a solution to the vampire side-effect and then he would have no reservation about owning a private island, enormous yacht and Lear jet, but until that time he was more than happy to be painting skirting boards with the woman he loved. He looked at Natasha who was standing on a stepladder to paint a door frame and smiled to himself. She looked so angry when she concentrated.

Natasha was painting a tricky bit of the door frame, relieved that she'd nearly finished it without any mistakes and also that Peter had given her the opportunity to visit Kelly's apartment without him knowing about it. She knew he'd be angry if she told him, especially if she told him about hacking into Kelly's computer. He wanted her to try and forget what had happened, but she couldn't do that. She needed to know all the answers, not just the ones that other people thought she should know. Once she understood what it was all about and could really believe that Kelly wouldn't be coming back, then she could move on with her life. She still had nightmares: being drugged, bound and gagged at that pervert's mercy. What had really happened between them, and how was Sheryl involved? Now that Peter had given her an excuse not to stay over she could visit Kelly's apartment tonight and download his files onto the *Mickey Mouse* memory stick then go back to her mum's flat and put it on her own laptop. She could then wipe the memory stick and have it back in the drawer before Peter realised it was missing.

It was getting late and the fridge was empty; they hadn't moved in properly and it only contained milk for their drinks. Originally they'd intended to go out for a meal but, since Peter now needed time at the lab, he offered to drive Natasha to her mum's flat, telling her that he'd pick up a take-away later. She tried to refuse but he was adamant and she realised that any further objections would begin to look suspicious. She bit her tongue and accepted with as much good grace as she could manage. It meant that she'd have to go to her mum's flat first and then get a Merseyrail train back to the city centre, all of which would take time. Hopefully the downloading of Kelly's files shouldn't take too long and then she could take a train back to her mum's flat before the trains stopped for the night. She checked her watch and did a quick mental calculation. She needed to leave soon if she was to do the round trip and still have enough time in Kelly's apartment.

'OK Pete, let's tidy things away and you can run me over to me mum's.'

Peter was surprised by the sudden change of mind and he hadn't quite finished his piece of skirting board, but he readily agreed because it would give him more time to work at the lab. They cleared away the dust sheets and moved the furniture back into its correct positions. Under the coffee table there was a rolled up rug. Natasha begin to move it then realised it was heavier than she thought.

'Pete give me a hand with the *VORK*.'

'The what?'

'The rug—isn't that what it's called? I spotted it when I was on *e-bay*—look.' she unrolled the end where she expected the tag to be but it had been cut off. She gave Peter a questioning look. 'Where's the label?'

'Don't know. I think Rachel must have done that. Perhaps she didn't want people to know she'd bought it in IKEA?'

'Why?'

'To be perfectly honest, Tash, she was a bit of a snob about things like that.'

Natasha grunted; something about the rug and its missing label unnerved her. It was all she could think about on the car journey to her mum's, fiddling with the *Mickey Mouse* memory stick in her pocket. Peter was silent, his thoughts focused on his own immediate problem with his vampire mice.

Peter had just dropped her outside her mum's block of flats and was driving away when Michelle arrived carrying two shopping bags. Natasha had not intended to actually go to the flat, but to let Peter drive away then go straight to the station and take a train back into the city centre, but, now she was trapped. She helped her mum carry the shopping up the stairs to the flat; the lift was still broken; with luck her mum would be back in her old flat in a week or two. Natasha sat impatiently watching the clock as her mum gave her a brief synopsis of the last episode of 'Corrie'. She tried to sound interested but all she could think about was how time was slipping by and, with it, her opportunity to visit Kelly's apartment secretly. At last, her mum checked her watch and announced that she was going to Bingo with her friend Maggie, and asked Natasha if she wanted to come too. Natasha made her excuses and half an hour later was on the train back into Liverpool.

It was getting late and Peter was hungry. It had taken much longer than he'd expected to falsify his results, but they now showed that the early results had been promising but that, as the trial had progressed, the mice had slowly begun to deteriorate. The results now made no mentioned of his second retro virus, the one that reversed the effects of the first. It had taken much longer than he'd expected. He couldn't alter one result without having to tinker with all the other ones; toxicology; histology and haematology all needed to agree with one another. He'd been very thorough and was now certain that if the department chose to check them they would be convinced that the trial had been a dismal failure.

Now all he had to do was inoculate the mice. He had a small batch of the second retro virus in the lab fridge; it was labelled as a control, meaning that it had no effect. He couldn't risk the chance that one of his colleagues might use it for some other trial and that his ruse might be detected. He would need to dispose of it afterwards, together with the syringes that he would use to inject the mice. He went into the stores and took out a dozen small disposable syringes, one for each mice on the trial, carefully filling them from the bottle of retro virus. The amount wasn't important; you could easily inoculate an adult human with the volumes he was using. He laid the filled syringes out on the bench in front of him—he could have used one large syringe and inoculated all the mice from it, but that would have gone against his training which was to avoid cross-contamination at all costs. It seemed stupid to be so careful since he was effectively killing the mice, but he took pride in doing things correctly. On a more practical note, it also meant that he wouldn't miss out any of the mice. Once he'd used all twelve syringes, he would know that he'd treated all the mice.

Peter lined up the cages and put on his thick gardening gloves, then he paused for a moment and looked at the mice; once he did this there was no going back. By next week he could be looking for another job, but at least he wouldn't be responsible for creating any human vampires. What would they be like he wondered? Based on his *psycho mice* they wouldn't look any different from a normal person, no fangs, no changing into bats, just aggressive and lusting for blood. Suddenly he felt a shiver run down his back. On the night that Natasha had been abducted he'd had another of his hallucinations: her parrot, had told him to take a message to the couple in 13C. After the event, when Natasha had been released and the case had been dropped, he'd thought no more about it. He'd accepted Sheryl's explanation that it was too do with Bob's past, that they were working for the government, that it was something 'hush-hush'. He'd assumed that when they called the man in black, Kelly, a 'vampire' it was an expression, not a description. But what if he really *was* a vampire? What if he'd done something to Natasha when he had her on her own? She'd certainly been different since that night. Perhaps it wasn't post-traumatic stress after all but something more sinister? She was often aggressive and talked to her dead nan all the time and seemed constantly preoccupied. He tried to dismiss the idea from his mind—it was just too fanciful too far-fetched. But, after all he was a scientist. If it could happen to mice then why not to humans? And wasn't it because of this possibility that he was risking his future by falsifying his results?

Peter worked methodically through the mice, taking each one from its cage and holding it steady with the thick gardening gloves while he injected it in the leg muscle, then replacing it in the cage. The virus didn't need to go into a vein; it would be absorbed through the muscle. Injecting into the muscle was less risky and produced less obvious bruising. Within a few days they would begin to deteriorate and by the time of their post-mortems there would be no sign of the injection site. He'd just reached the last cage when he realised that he had two syringes left; then he remembered the mouse that he'd dissected, which was why there were only eleven left. He was about to dispose of the extra syringe when he thought about his earlier concerns over Natasha and placed it in his coat pocket. He knew he was being stupid or hoped he was, but he intended to destroy the remaining retro virus, and he didn't want to have cause to regret that decision.

He put the gloves back on and opened the last cage. This mouse seemed more placid than the others but he was still careful picking it up. He held it in his hand and injected it in the leg.

'Oww! For fucks sake—why did you do that?'

He dropped the syringe and the mouse. It landed back in the open cage and started rubbing its hind leg with it front paw.

'What?'

'I thought we were friends?'

'Friends?'

'Will you stop repeating me, I've told you about it before—it's actually quite irritating. Don't you remember me—Frank?'

'But you were a parrot?'

'Jesus, kid, do we have to go through this every time—I'm an angel *disguised* as a parrot.'

'You're a mouse?'

'OK—mouse…Look you've got me confused now. I *am* an angel; I *was* a pigeon—and now I'm a mouse.'

'Pigeon?'

'Yes—a pigeon, I've got one on 'pause' sitting outside. I just changed into a mouse so we could have a little chat in private.'

'Why?'

'Because, I'm fond of you kid and I don't want anything to happen to you.'

'Look—I know you're just another hallucination brought on by stress. First it was a pigeon with a sore leg, then a drunk parrot, then a seagull and now a psycho-mouse. You're all figments of my imagination. I'm sure it'd be fun to chat, but I'm not Doctor Dolittle and I'm in a hurry!'

Peter slammed the cage shut and locked it.

'What?!' The mouse was standing on its hind legs holding the bars of the cage, 'You ungrateful little shit. I come here to save you and you stab me in the leg and lock me up.'

Peter smiled. 'I thought you were my guardian angel. Isn't that what *you* do—save people?'

'I *was* your guardian angel but I've been transferred. They gave me the night off. Thought I'd come and keep an eye on you—don't know why I bothered.'

'Why would you do that?'

'Well kid, I've got quite fond of you, and until I get reassigned I thought I'd try and keep you safe. It's only happened once before—and it didn't end well.'

'What happened last time?'

'She died.'

Peter felt cold. He knew the answer to the next question but he asked it all the same. 'You mean Rachel?'

The mouse nodded. 'Sorry kid, I lied when I said I was there and it was an accident. I don't know what happened. One day I'm looking out for her; then I get a day off; the next day she's dead and I've been given you to look after.'

'But why me? Why not Rachel?'

'Perhaps it was because of the child. You two get together and they think the child is the one they want. Then she gets pregnant and they realise it's the wrong child so they get rid of her and the child and wait for you to find someone else—better luck next time.'

'You make it sound like an experiment—like we're lab animals, not people.'

The mouse shrugged. 'You can't make an omelette without breaking a few eggs.'

'Why are they moving you to another assignment?'

'Perhaps this one is the right child and they don't need you any longer. We're short of man-power so we can't look after every waif and stray.'

'Child? What child?'

'Yours! Yours and Natasha's.'

'Natasha's pregnant?'

'Jesus—are you really so dumb? Why do you think she's been acting so strangely? She's worried you'll leave her when you know—like her dad did.'

'I thought she was a vampire.'

The mouse shook its head and sighed. 'No wonder I worry about you.'

'But, what if it's *not* the right child?'

'What?'

'Perhaps they sent you here to keep me busy while they have her killed.'

'No! I told you, kid: they don't know I'm here. Let's just stay here; we'll have a nice chat and I'll make sure you're OK.'

'But, you lied before. Why should I believe you now? I need to talk to Tash—now.'

Peter grabbed his coat and car keys. The mouse called after him until it heard the car driving away. There was no way that he could follow him by pigeon and gulls were like taxis, you could never find one this time of night. It sat on its wheel and rubbed its leg.

'Frank old lad,' it muttered to itself, 'you should know by now: the secret to making omelettes is not to get too fond of the eggs.'

Peter drove to Michelle's apartment but it was all in darkness. He could have rung the bell but it was late and he didn't want to wake them up and make a scene. After all, how would he explain having a conversation with a laboratory mouse without appearing deranged? His hallucinations were to do with stress, he was sure of it. He'd go back to his apartment, get a good night's rest then he could talk things through with Natasha in the morning. That would be the time to find out if she really was pregnant or if that was another figment of his overactive imagination.

He picked up a curry on the way back to the apartment and was sitting at the breakfast bar eating it and drinking a cold beer. It was very late but he was too hungry to go to bed. He put his hand in his coat pocket to check his phone for messages and found the small syringe of retro virus, smiled and put it on the side; to think he'd seriously thought that Natasha was a vampire. He sipped his beer and took another bite from his naan bread, then the intercom buzzed. Perhaps it was Natasha? She was always forgetting her keys. He swallowed his food, walked over to the wall-mounted intercom and pressed the button.

'Hello?'

'Hello, I'm sorry it's so late sir' said the metallic voice of the intercom. 'P C Mackintosh here, Merseyside Police. I've some bad news for you. Do you mind if I come up?'

Peter panicked, it must be about Natasha. He pressed the button opening the outside door.

4

HILTON HOTEL

It was a lazy spring morning; she'd just visited her hairdresser and had arranged to meet her sister in twenty minutes' time for a mid-morning cappuccino. St Mark's Square was already quite busy. Groups of foreign tourists were taking photographs of each other and feeding the pigeons. Why did they do that? Pigeons were vermin; it was like taking a picture of yourself with a rat.

Venice never altered; only the faces and the clothes changed; the buildings, like her, remained the same. She closed her eyes and remembered how she'd experienced this square for first time, as a child. She opened them half expecting to see beggars and soldiers but saw only a long line of Chinese schoolchildren in identical uniforms clutching guide books. She pushed her way through them and felt the frisson of young blood. Crossing the square towards *Florian's*, the waiter saw her and beckoned her to an empty table, which was on the edge of the square directly in front of the restaurant. The table was slightly in the shade and close to a string quartet who were entertaining the patrons; she always sat at this table, it gave her an uninterrupted view of her territory.

'*Buongiorno*, Contessa,' said the waiter, 'you are alone?'

She nodded. 'The usual, Giuseppe, and the *New York Times.*'

He returned with the paper held in a wooden frame and a small cappuccino. She sipped the cappuccino and opened the paper. She found modern news so boring and mundane but it helped to practice her English. There was no use speaking five languages if you couldn't read them too, and it was always wise to have some understanding of current events. She checked her watch, the gold and diamonds glinting in the pale spring sun, and adjusted her sunglasses then suddenly sensed her sister approaching from behind. Turning to acknowledge her sister, she was surprised to see a man dressed in black who walked past her table and took a seat a few tables away.

Laying the newspaper on the empty seat beside her, she pushed the sunglasses to the end of her nose and studied him. He was dressed entirely in black and wore a large hat and gloves even though it was mild for the time of year. His hair was quite long, covering his ears and he wore large sunglasses, which made it impossible to tell if he was studying her in return. She smiled to herself, sipped her coffee—and waited.

The waiter took the man's order and as he passed her table, she touched his arm.

'Giuseppe, who is that man?' she asked.

'He is no one, Contessa—an American tourist.'

'Ask him to join me.'

'Contessa?'

She gave the waiter an icy stare; he knew not to question her and hurried to pass on the message. The stranger seemed unsurprised. He rose and walked casually towards her, stopping in front of her table.

'Contessa?—is that correct? You wanted to see me?'

She held out her hand but didn't rise. 'Welcome to Venice *brother*, and you are?'

'Stephen Patrick Kelly, ma'am—but everyone calls me Steve.' Kelly made a slight bow, took her hand kissed it.

'An American and a gentleman—two surprises in one.' She smiled and moved her newspaper, patting the chair, 'Please take a seat, Stephen.'

The waiter arrived with Kelly's coffee which he laid on the table cloth. She waved him away. 'Thank you Giuseppe, that will be all,'

She waited until he'd left. 'Now Stephen, what is the purpose of your visit, is it business or pleasure?'

Kelly looked over her shoulder at the Chinese school-children. 'Both.'

She turned, saw what he was looking and laughed. 'We Venetians pride ourselves on our hospitality, I am sure something can be arranged for your amusement—but what of the business?'

'I have a problem with some other *family* back home.'

'America?'

'Liverpool, England. A man called Melville and a woman called Malone.'

She sat a little further upright in her chair but tried not to appear too curious: 'Melville?'

'I've known him since the beginning in 1862. He *made* me—then I *made* her, fifty years ago.'

'When was *he* made?'

'Don't know—we've never had the chance to reminisce.'

Kelly was looking over her shoulder again. She wasn't used to this and felt slightly annoyed; she was usually centre of attention as far as men were concerned, an advantage of staying young and beautiful indefinitely. Perhaps because of her beauty, men had always underestimated her and many had died as a result. But then again, perhaps Kelly wasn't interested in women after all. She turned half expecting to see an attractive young man but saw a familiar figure instead—now she understood. Everyone had their Achilles heel,—even a vampire like Kelly. Perhaps she could use that knowledge to her advantage?

Kelly was distracted, a young girl was walking across the square in their direction. She was perfect *soft centre* material, probably mid-teens, quite thin with pale skin and long straight blonde hair. She reminded Kelly of someone, but who? Then he remembered and smiled to himself—*Alice in Wonderland*. 'Alice' continued to walk towards them. She stopped next to the table.

'Stephen, may I introduce my sister, Eloise.'

Kelly half stood and held out his hand. 'Please to meet you, signorina.'

Eloise giggled and curtsied.

'Eloise, this is our American *brother* Mr Kelly,' said the Contessa. 'He has been entertaining me with tales of England. It is so many years since we were last there—perhaps we should visit again?'

That evening Kelly waited on the landing stage next to his hotel smoking a cigarette. He checked his watch then saw a sleek mahogany motor-launch approaching. It pulled in alongside the jetty.

'Mister Stephen?' asked the boatman. Kelly flicked his cigarette into the canal and climbed aboard.

The boat drew away from the hotel and turned onto the Grand Canal. It was a short journey first down the main canal and then through a myriad of smaller tributaries. Kelly became slightly disorientated and then on his guard, realising that this was deliberate so that he wouldn't be able to easily retrace his steps either back to his hotel or to revisit his destination if the meeting ahead went badly. He was very aware that he was on another vampire's territory, and that could often be a very dangerous place to be.

The Contessa had appeared friendly enough but he had no intention being naive. He'd looked into her eyes and seen a reflection of himself—another predator. Perhaps her invitation was an elaborate ruse, a way to get him alone and dispose of him. He felt vulnerable because he was unarmed. He'd decided not to risk bringing a gun through customs; a razor would have been ideal but he'd lost his somewhere in Liverpool.

The boat turned into a dark and small side canal. It drew in alongside a small archway where the boatman tied up to a large wooden post before cutting the engine and jumping ashore. He held out his hand to help Kelly then pushed a bell next to a large wooden door which immediately opened, illuminating them in a bright shaft of light.

The Contessa was waiting at the doorway.

'Welcome Stephen. It is cold on the water tonight—please come this way.'

Kelly followed her down a small dimly lit hallway into a large reception room; the ceiling was high and two chandeliers hung from the ornately carved rafters. Oil paintings hung on two of the walls, a marble fireplace with roaring log fire dominated another while at the far end of the room a long mahogany table had been set with three places. The gold candlesticks and cutlery glinted under the candlelight.

Kelly understood that his arrival through the rear entrance and into these palatial surroundings was designed to impress—and he was impressed; but he was also amused that the Contessa had felt it necessary to do it. He smiled to himself; vanity was obviously her weakness. Perhaps he could find some way to exploit that.

She suggested that he should warm himself by the fire and went to get some drinks. When she returned he was studying a large oil painting of a young woman with a view of the Rialto Bridge in the background. Although its surface was crazed with the passage of time the subject was still instantly recognisable.

'It doesn't do you justice, Contessa.'

'You flatter me Stephen. He was the Doge's personal artist and many still consider him a genius.'

'Genius or not, he hasn't captured your beauty.'

She smiled and handed him a glass of champagne.

'To blood brothers,' she said as they clinked the glasses.

'And sisters,' Kelly replied.

Kelly was enjoying the evening immensely. The Contessa was an excellent hostess and he flirted with Eloise much to the Contessa amusement. They explained that their staff had been given the evening off so that they could be candid without the possibility of being overheard. Consequently, they'd arranged for a local restaurant to supply the food and, since they had no idea of Kelly's tastes, the wide variety of dishes could best be described as 'international'.

The two women were such good company that Kelly began to relax. It had been a long time since he'd been able to be so open about his life. He did most of the talking and it was only later that he realised that they had been careful not to give too much away of their own pasts.

He was curious about one thing though.

'If you are a contessa? Shouldn't there be a conte or is it count?' he asked.

'You are correct, Stephen. There was a conte—my dear Luca. He was young and so vigorous—a tragic accident took him from me.'

'What happened?'

'He drowned.'

'In his bath,' giggled her sister.

Kelly smiled, 'Ah,—a conveniently tragic accident?'

'Quite so Stephen. He left me a fortune and a title.'

'And this house?'

'Oh no, this has been owned by my family since it was built—although we have not lived here for many years. We would be too conspicuous if we stayed here too long. Venice is a small city and everyone knows everyone else's business. Soon we will have to find pastures new. It is curse we all bare—is it not Stephen?'

'I suppose it is.'

'Would you recommend this Liverpool of yours?'

Kelly laughed, 'Well it's getting a bit crowded at the moment.'

'With your Melville and Malone?' She purposely pronounced Melville as though it was unfamiliar to her.

'There's also an associate of mine, called Dean.'

'Perhaps you should arrange a few tragic accidents of your own?'

Kelly laughed. 'I don't think I've got a big enough bath.'

The Contessa shared a secret smile with her sister and nodded almost imperceptibly towards her handbag.

They'd just finished their meal and Kelly was smoking a cigar and savouring an excellent port when suddenly the Contessa began to cough and appeared to be fighting for her breath. She leaned over the table wheezing. Eloise jumped up and put her arm around her shoulders.

Kelly rushed to her side. 'What is it?'

'There must have been shellfish in the food—she's allergic.' Eloise waved at her sister's handbag on a side table, 'Please get it for me.'

Kelly brought her the handbag and she pulled out a strange object like an orange marker pen. 'An adrenalin injection to stop the anaphylaxis,' explained Eloise. 'Please hold her arm.'

Kelly held the Contessa's arm still and Eloise pulled the cap off the syringe then she plunged it into Kelly's arm.

'What the fuc- ?' Eloise smiled at him while his body began to shake and his muscles went into spasm. He fell backwards onto the floor, then he was laying on his back, staring up at the chandelier hanging from the ceiling; aware of his surrounding but unable to move a muscle. The two women stared disdainfully down at him.

'Men are such fools,' said the Contessa now fully recovered. Eloise giggled.

They knelt on either side of his body and began to search him. He cursed himself for being so stupid. What made him think a vampire could be allergic to anything? He realised that they intended to kill him and a perverse part of his mind wondered what they had planned for him. He could feel their hands touching his body but he was locked inside his head, staring up at the ceiling. He felt them open his shirt and he saw a hand with a bejewelled Arabian dagger. The hand moved out of his line of sight. He tried to flinch in anticipation of the first cut—but his body wouldn't respond. He waited and waited. He could hear faint indistinct voices as though they were discussing where to begin. He knew how they felt; he'd often felt like this before a kill: the anticipation was almost unbearable but once you had a helpless victim it was sometimes difficult to decide where to start. After what seemed an eternity his view of the chandelier was suddenly obscured by the silhouette of a head and he smelled perfume and with a sense of detachment wondered if they planned to decapitate him.

The Contessa leaned over him so that her face was close to his.

'Stephen, we have given you a tranquilliser, such as veterinarians give to large predators. I hope you take that as a compliment—it is meant as one. If we wished you dead I would already have cut out your heart—it would not be the first time, and as the tranquilliser has no anaesthetic properties, that would have been most unpleasant for you. However, as we have found you a most diverting dinner companion we have decided to let you live—do you understand?'

She reached down and removed his sunglasses and suddenly everything was brighter.

'Ah, so this is why you dress as you do,' she said. 'Was this this due to your vendetta in Liverpool? Soon the drug will clear and we can talk.'

It took twenty minutes for Kelly to regain full use of his limbs. They sat him in a chair by the fire; his artificial hand lay on the table by his side, together with his sunglasses. He felt vulnerable and violated, emotions he'd not experienced since his days in reform school and which he had hoped never to feel again. For their part the two women seemed embarrassed by their actions and very contrite.

The Contessa handed him a large glass of brandy.

'Please, do not be angry with us, Stephen. We are only protecting ourselves as we have for many years. Once we have shared some of our past with you then perhaps you will understand. We may even be able to be of assistance to you with your *family* problems?'

Kelly sat in silence, unsure how to react and the Contessa began to relate her life story. Kelly then began to tell them how the vendetta with Melville and Malone had begun, how he had sustained his injuries and what had just taken place in Liverpool. Once he'd finished the Contessa placed her hand on his arm.

'Thank you Stephen for your honesty,' she said. 'I must admit that when we first met this morning I was not entirely honest with you myself. I have met your Mr Melville before, many years ago. Once I have explained the circumstances you will appreciate that it may be beneficial to both our causes that we form an alliance.'

Kelly still felt angered by the events of the evening and his own stupidity, but he was eager to hear more of Melville's past. He decided to wait for a suitable moment to avenge himself for his humiliation at their hands.

A short while later, the boatman returned to take him back to his hotel. He sat silently in the back of the boat and tried to make sense of his situation. Had they really let him live because they found him amusing? That was possible; he'd done it himself in the past, but somehow it didn't ring true. He'd only done it with victims, not with other vampires. That sort of mistake could come back to bite you—he smiled at his turn of phrase.

The following morning Kelly was up early but still tired, the result of the drug and a restless night's sleep. He'd learned so much last evening about his hosts and about their past, including much about Melville, but he knew not to trust either of them. Why were they so keen to visit Liverpool? It was a tempting proposition never the less; he'd love to see the look on Melville's face when those two appeared. And how would Malone react to the competition? Kelly laughed out loud; he could never resist temptation.

They'd arranged to meet for lunch in St Mark's Square at noon. Kelly showered, ordered a light breakfast from room service and was laying out his clothes on the bed when he realised that his shirts were in a different order in the wardrobe to the one he'd hung them in, an easy mistake because they were all black, but he knew the difference. So that was what the boatman had been doing while they were eating—he'd been searching Kelly's room. The Contessa and her sister had gone to some lengths to find out about him; perhaps he should repay the compliment? He rang room service and cancelled his breakfast and within ten minutes he was outside the hotel with a guide book and a map of the city. He needed to find the house where they'd entrapped him and find out more about them. He checked his watch—four hours until they were due to meet. By then he hoped to have a better idea of who he was dealing with.

Kelly leaned on the wooden rail of the hotel landing stage and examined the map. He'd visited Venice before and he understood the basic geography of the city and was thus able to roughly work out which area of the city he'd visited the previous night, despite the circuitous route taken by the boatman. And on the return journey he'd made a mental note of the route. The boatman must have assumed that Kelly was disorientated and no longer a threat because he'd made fewer detours from the main canals on the way back to Kelly's hotel.

Within an hour, Kelly had located the house, although 'palace' might be a more appropriate description. The previous evening he'd been delivered to the tradesman's entrance but the opposite side of the building had a grand marble entrance opening onto a small canal lined by restaurants and elegant boutiques. Kelly chose a small restaurant that overlooking the marble entrance and ordered breakfast. He looked at the evening menu on the wall and recognised many of the dishes from the previous evening. No doubt this was where the food had come from that had apparently 'poisoned' the Contessa.

He ate his breakfast; watched and waited. The waiter told him that the house was occupied by a Russian Princess who'd married a local Count, but the waiter didn't know her name—they just called her 'the Contessa'. Kelly finished his breakfast and since there was still no sign of life opposite, he decided to pursue his investigations elsewhere.

Half an hour later he was in the 'Accademia' art gallery, studying a portrait. A guide was taking a group on a tour through the gallery and Kelly joined them, the guide was explaining the history and significance of each of the pictures in the room. The subject of the portrait was of no interest to Kelly but the artist's style was familiar. Kelly interrupted the guide.

'Have you got any others?'

'Sorry?' the guide seemed puzzled by the question.

'Did he paint any other Venetians?'

'Oh yes—he was a genius but most prolific. He painted many of the aristocracy of Venice—we have several examples in the gallery. Shall we move on to the next room?'

'What about the others? Do you know who else he painted?'

The guide didn't appreciate a foreigner questioning her knowledge; they were usually so passive.

'I believe we have a book about him in the gift shop,' she said dismissively.

Kelly bowed, touched his large black hat and left the gallery. A few minutes later he was sitting in a restaurant by the Accademia Bridge with a large coffee table book on his lap looking at colour plates of portraits held by the galleries around the world. The artist's style was unmistakable, and he had been the Doge's personal artist. He came to a section entitled 'Lost Masterpieces'. There was no photograph of the picture but there was a full description: Portrait of young woman from Venice with view of Rialto Bridge (approx. 1478) believed to be Isabella Foscari. Owned by Isaac Stein and confiscated by the Nazis' in 1939—believed destroyed Berlin 1945.

He now had a name and an address and was looking forward to his lunch.

§

Dean lay in bed smoking a joint and feeling frustrated and confused. It was now three weeks since he'd been shot in the lift and although he'd completely recovered physically he felt that something was different about him.

The last thing he remembered of that day was having a smoke in the lift while waiting for Kelly to search the apartment; then that fat bastard had burst through the fire door and shot him. He touched the side of his chest; the wound had completely healed; there wasn't even a scar. It still felt sore though.

The next thing he remembered was waking up in hospital, handcuffed to the bed with a bizzie sitting in the chair next to him. Then that fuckin' DI had tried to get him to talk, threatened him with prison. Dean had been to a young offender's institution for car theft. It had not been a pleasant experience and one he had no desire to repeat. However he was more frightened of Kelly than he was of a few months inside and he had no intention of grassing on anyone, let alone a mad bastard like Kelly. He kept his mouth shut. After a few more visits the cuffs were removed and the charges were dropped. He still didn't understand that part; perhaps Kelly had connections or had bribed someone. Whatever the reason he was left alone to recover which he did surprisingly quickly and now he was back at home with his mother. There'd been no communication from Kelly or his brother Lewis since the shooting. Perhaps they were laying low until they were sure he wasn't under surveillance by the police.

Dean took a last drag of his joint and stubbed it out in the ashtray by his bed.

'Wait 'til I see that fucker Wayne –told me that shite wer the best skunk,' he grumbled. He pulled on his clothes and shuffled to the bathroom and then the living room where his mother was sitting on the sofa with her back to him, watching the TV.

"Bout fuckin' time—thought yer'd died in ther" she said without turning around. 'Betta get yer arse in gear if yer gonna get t' the Job Centre t' sign on.'

'Mornin' Ma,' Dean switched on the kettle and scratched his crotch.

'If they stop yer benefits don't come to me fer owt—I'm strapped for cash meself. Youse two are always spongin' off me.'

Dean made himself a mug of tea then sat down next to her on the sofa.

'What's on?' He nodded at the TV.

'Fuck all.'

He stretched out and took a cigarette from the packet on the coffee table then took the cigarette from his mother's hand and used it to light his.

'Thanks Ma—I'll 'av this brew then shoot off.'

'D'yer want summin' to eat first?'

'Nah, no worries—feel like 'm gonna puke me guts up.'

'Charmin'—must be coz of all the ale yer spent yer dole on.'

'Nah—feel like this every mornin'—since I got outta hossie.'

'There's a parcel on the side fer yer. Cud be from Lewis; God knows wer 'e's buggered off to. Not a word ter 'is ma fer three weeks an' me worried 'death 'bout 'im.'

Dean stretched over, picked up a small 'jiffy' bag and read the address.

'Why d'yer think its fer me, Ma?'

'Coz it sez Dean, an' flat 85—yer divvy.'

'Sez Tweedle-Dean?—cud be someone else's.'

'Who the fuck cares—it cud be worth summin'.'

Dean ripped open the parcel. Inside there was a bundle of twenty-pound notes and a small mobile phone.

§

Kelly had only been back in Liverpool for a few days and he was looking for somewhere to stay. He'd originally intended to travel to the States from Italy and lay low for a few months while he decided what to do about Melville and Malone. However, since meeting the Contessa he'd decided that the opportunity to make use of her was too good to pass up. There was definitely some history between her and Melville and, although he hadn't been able to find out too many details, he was sure that it wouldn't be good news for the 'dynamic duo'. If he played his cards right things could work out perfectly for him—but he still thought it was wise to keep away from Rumford Court. They would probably be keeping an eye on it for any signs of his reappearance.

When he'd left Malone and the red-haired girl at his apartment he'd driven straight to the industrial unit in Birkenhead; he'd needed time to think and he had Lewis's body to dispose of. He'd originally intended to dump it in the Mersey, either that or leave it in the 4X4 and set fire to it. However, on further consideration he'd decided that a body, whether burned or water-logged, would only provoke a more thorough police investigation whereas, if Lewis just disappeared, they wouldn't exert themselves even if they continued looking for him. He wasn't sure if the police had details of the 4X4 so he kept it hidden under a tarpaulin in the industrial unit. Lewis's body was more difficult to conceal because it had begun to smell. Kelly, who had plenty of experience of disposing of bodies, decided to resort to Nitric Acid to make Lewis's disappearance total. He'd lifted the body into an old enamel bath in the shower room at the industrial unit, filled the bath with acid and put a weight on the body's chest to keep it submerged—then he took the next flight from Liverpool airport, which had just happened to be to Venice.

On his return he'd gone straight to the industrial unit. There was no evidence that the police had been there: the 4X4 was still under the tarpaulin and all that remained of Lewis was thick brown scum on the surface of the acid. He used heavy-duty rubber gloves and a long handled sieve to check for any traces of his body and found only a gold crown from one of his teeth and a gold earring that he'd forgotten to remove earlier. He locked up the unit and took a Merseyrail train under the Mersey and north out of the city; he was going back to familiar territory. His Venetian guests would arrive in a few days and he needed somewhere to lay low and make his plans in peace.

The following morning, after an indifferent breakfast at his hotel, he was staring in an Estate Agent's window looking for an apartment to let. He was in Southport, twenty miles north of the city, far enough away that he was unlikely to encounter Melville or Malone but close enough that he could keep them under surveillance when he wanted to. He was impatient to find somewhere suitable but all the apartments in Southport looked similar and although his gang had run this town before his murder he didn't know the geography of it very well. Then he spotted something surprising in the Estate Agent's window, He laughed out loud and entered.

'Hiya, can I help you love?' asked the receptionist.

'I hope so.' Kelly smiled. 'The one-bedroom apartment in the window—is that really the address?'

'Lathom Road? Yes—why?'

'I knew someone called Lathom once.'

'Was he a friend?'

'More of a business acquaintance. Do you think I could have a viewing?'

§

The following afternoon Dean was on a Merseyrail train heading north out of the city. He was in good spirits, he had money in his pocket and he was looking forward to seeing his brother Lewis again. He remembered when they were kids and used to skive off school and take this train to the seaside. The truancy officer came around a few times but eventually got fed up being told to 'fuck off' by Ma, and left them alone, and their school decided that they were more trouble to have around and so didn't pursue the matter. Consequently, their last few years at school had been more about 'hot wiring' cars on the estate and riding the trains than attending lessons—that was until Dean was caught in a stolen car and ended up doing six months inside.

The train pulled into Southport Station. As he walked towards the barrier Dean suddenly had an urge to run up to it and vault over like they used to do when they were kids. He resisted the temptation—he'd paid for his ticket.

The message on the mobile phone in the 'jiffy bag' had given him precise instructions. As he was early for the meeting he bought himself an ice cream and sat in King's Gardens. Usually he'd have sat in a pub and had few beers but he just didn't fancy it. Alcohol didn't seem to affect him any longer and it tasted strange as well. Perhaps it was due to all the drugs they'd given him in hospital? He watched some young boys try to break a climbing frame and though of Lewis; it'd be good to see him again. Dean finished his ice cream, checked his watch and walked slowly through the park and on towards the Pier. The sun was beginning to set and its large orange disk sank slowly towards the horizon; he walked down the pier in the opposite direction to everyone else. At the far end a lone fisherman was silhouetted against the sky. The man was sitting with his back to him, an empty folding chair next to him. The instructions had been precise—Dean sat in the vacant seat.

'Evening Dean.' Kelly stared straight ahead and wound in the slack of his line.

'Hiya Mr K,' Dean looked around. 'Where's Lew?'

'Dead.'

'Wot!?'

'Sorry—I suppose that's what I'm expected to say, is it?'

'Yeah, s'pose,' Dean stared at his feet; he was shaken.

'How?'

'She cut his throat.

'Who?'

'The Malone girl.'

'Why?'

'Does it matter? Let's move on—I've a job for you Dean.'

'Gonna get *me* killed now?'

Kelly laughed: 'No—I made sure that's not going to happen.'

'How?'

'I'll tell you, but you won't believe me—yet.'

An hour later Dean was on the return journey, clutching a parcel and more confused than when he'd first arrived. He already knew that Kelly was psycho but now he knew Kelly was a definitely a nutter as well. Kelly wanted him to believe that Kelly, Melville and the Malone girl were all vampires, drank blood and could live forever—and that Kelly had made him a vampire too. That, apparently, was why he'd survived after being shot in the lift and why he'd recovered so quickly. Dean looked at his reflection in the train window, pulled up his lip and checked his teeth. Shouldn't they be pointy? Kelly was full of shit. He stretched out his feet on the seat opposite, closed his eyes and tried to catch up on his sleep.

He'd been finding it difficult to sleep since he'd come out of hospital, no doubt due to all those drugs they'd pumped him full of. They probably gave him someone else's drugs by mistake, or some experimental shit—you couldn't trust the NHS. Dean couldn't see any other way to explain why he felt sick every morning and starving the rest of the day. No matter how much he ate, it was never enough to stop the craving for food. The only thing that seemed to help was exercise. He'd started working out with some old weights and after only two weeks had a six pack and was beginning to look like a body builder. Perhaps the drugs the hospital had given him were turning him into the Incredible Hulk. Perhaps he wouldn't complain after all, not unless he turned green and then he'd make them pay for a spray tan.

He was just dozing off and hoping that he didn't have one of those weird dreams again, the ones where he craved blood, trying to clear his mind and forget about the blood, when he became aware of someone else in the carriage. He opened his eyes intending to tell them to 'fuck off.'

Lewis was sitting on the seat opposite. Dean jumped half out of his skin.

'Lew? Kelly sed yer woz dead.'

'I am, Dean—she cut me 'ere to 'ere.' Lewis traced his finger across his throat.

The vision disappeared and Dean was alone again.

The train had stopped at a station and the doors were still open. Dean ran onto the platform and stood there shaking and when the train doors closed and the train pulled away, he was still there, sitting on a bench and trying to collect his thoughts, trying to make sense out of what had just happened.

'Then she drank me blood.'

Dean turned. Lewis was sitting on the bench next to him; he screamed and leapt to his feet and the vision disappeared. He looked along the platform where a smattering of passengers were staring at him and his empty bench, then he walked to the end of the platform as far away from the bench as possible. He looked at the parcel that Kelly had given him. It was a large 'jiffy' bag and he knew it contained a considerable amount of money; he'd been told to get himself a gun and Kelly another car. Kelly seemed to think his old American 4X4 might be recognised and had stipulated that the new car had to be an automatic and different.

After fifteen minutes, the next train arrived, and Dean got hesitantly on board. Three stops later he left the train feeling much calmer and set off for home. He'd just crossed the railway bridge where he'd first met Kelly and was heading towards his block of flats when a black BMW screeched to a halt in front of him.

'Oh, fuck!' he muttered under his breath.

Three men got out of the car and blocked his path.

'Wer' yer bin i-din'?' asked the man with the gold chains.

'No wer—just got outta hossie, like. Got shot—didn't yer 'ere?'

'Who woz it—pest control?' they all laughed, even Dean.

'That's a gud'n Moxy,' Dean gave a weak smile, 'Pest control—yeah.'

'Shut the fuck up, dog breath,' the man poked him in the chest, 'I'll tell yer when to laugh—OK?'

Dean put up his hands. 'OK—Moxy—no offence like.'

'Werz that runt of a brother of yers?'

'Lewis?'

'Course fuckin' Lewis, yer knob head. How many fuckin' brothers have yer got?'

''E's gone away.'

'Run away with me fuckin' money more like. Search 'im lads.'

'Look Moxy 'm broke—waitin' fer me giro. Lewis'll pay yer when he getz back—honest.'

The other men grabbed Dean and went through his pockets. They handed the 'jiffy' bag to Moxy.

'Holdin' out of me yer little shite. What's this smack?'

'Give it back Moxy; it don't belong to me. I'll be in deep shit if I lose that.'

Moxy ripped open the 'jiffy' bag and looked at the bundle of notes.

'Tryin' to con me yer fuckin arse 'ole!—'It 'im boys.'

One of the men held Dean's arms behind his back and the other hit him hard in the stomach—but he didn't crumple as expected, so they hit him again, this time near his chest wound. The sharp pain unleashed something in Dean, something he had no control over. He tore free of the man's grip and head-butted the other man in the face. As he fell to the ground, the second man pulled a knife so Dean hit him in the solar plexus with his elbow then seized him by the hair and smashed his head against the car windscreen, smashing it. Moxy backed away, fumbling in his coat pocket but Dean was too quick. He grabbed Moxy by the throat, lifted him up in the air and threw him across the pavement and through a shop window, Moxy's gun clattered to the floor at Dean's feet.

Dean picked up the bundle of notes and put them in his pocket together with the gun. In the past he would have run away, but now he felt strangely calm. The two men were groaning on the pavement while Moxy lay slumped half in and half out of the shop window. A large sliver of glass had severed Moxy's neck and blood bubbled from the wound. Dean was overcome by a compelling urge to taste the blood; he leaned over and lapped at it like a cat with a bowl of cream. His dreams of blood had appalled him; the reality was different. He revelled in the taste, felt invigorated by it. A warm glow spread throughout his body and he drank his fill before walking slowly back to his flat.

The following morning he was up bright and early. He felt different, as though he was seeing the world for the first time. He left the flat before his mother was awake. Kelly had trusted him with the money and had given him instructions and he had no intention of letting him down. He now had Moxy's gun in his pocket, which was no doubt illegal and couldn't be linked to his murder; that only left him the car to find. He counted the bundle of notes, peeled off a few for expenses and hailed a cab.

Half an hour later he was outside a non-descript industrial unit on the other side of the city. He paid the cab driver and entered without knocking. A man in breathing apparatus was spraying paint on a car's wing. He continued to spray until he'd finished then he took off the mask.

'You'va fuckin' cheek cumin 'ere, yer little shite.'

'Don' be like that Eddy—I did'n grass yer up ter thur bizzies. I kept stumm—got six months like.'

'Well some arse'ole did—nearly ended up inside meself.'

'Weren't me Eddy—look've got a job fer yer. I need a car—clean not a bent one, an' I've got readies.'

Dean held out the bundle of notes. Eddy's mood changed immediately.

'Don' mind me Deano—musta got outta ther wrong side ov thur fuckin' bed. What do yer want anyhouse 'atchback or limo?'

'Summit big—he 'ad a black yank 4X4. Sed get summit different like.'

'Cum to right place Deano—I can deffo do different.'

§

Kelly was settling into his new apartment on the second floor of a converted Victorian house. He was savouring a celebratory bourbon and examining a knife that he'd bought in a junk shop that morning, a Kukri as used by the

Ghurkhas, this one dated to WW2. He drew it from its leather scabbard, weighed the heavy blade in his hand and contemplated his revenge on Melville and Malone. Re-sheathing the knife, he stood up, checked his watch and looked out of the window at the road outside. Where was he? A large vulgar and very white 4X4 pulled up. The door opened and Dean got out. Kelly spluttered into his glass.

'Fucking idiot!' he spat.

He took the lift to the ground floor and found Dean polishing the windscreen.

'Diya like it Mr K? It was owned by a footballer.'

Kelly was speechless. Dean was puzzled, but continued.

'White pearlescent paint, black roof with real gold flecks in the paint, 22" black alloy wheels an' best of all,' he opened the driver's door, 'tah dah—red leather interior an' a sound system that'll make yer ears bleed.'

'I said *different* Dean.'

'It is different Mr K.'

'Dean—it looks like a New Orleans whorehouse.'

Dean smiled. 'Yer 'ad me goin' thur Mr K—I thought yer didn' like it fer a bit.'

Kelly muttered something under his breath and went back to his bourbon; Dean smiled and carried on polishing the car.

§

A few days later Kelly was waiting in the terminal at John Lennon airport. He didn't normally do waiting because it tended to make him angry and when he was angry someone usually got hurt. However today was different; he was looking forward to this meeting, and even though the flight had been delayed he was still in good spirits.

He was idly watching a party of schoolchildren who had just come through the arrival gate and who were being rounded up by their teachers. They were milling around chattering, cases and trollies scattered everywhere. One of the teachers was trying desperately to count them. She'd attempted to have a roll-call but such was the excitement of her charges that she'd been ignored and instead she'd settled for a simple head count. But the children kept moving. She gave up and began to herd them towards the automatic doors and their waiting coach. Kelly was bored and mischievously wondered if she'd miss one?

Suddenly there was a commotion and his guests appeared through the arrival gate. Kelly nearly laughed out loud. The Contessa was leading a large group of officials. She appeared to be holding court, everyone was leaning close to her as though listening for instructions or pearls of wisdom. Two security guards were pushing trollies laden with cases. She was dressed in the style of a Fifties movie-star complete with mink coat while her sister trailed behind doing her Alice in Wonderland impression.

He stood up to greet her as the entourage approached. 'So much for a quiet entrance,' thought Kelly. She stopped in front of him and her followers ground to a halt around her. Looking first at her for instructions and then at him.

Kelly bowed slightly and touched his hat but didn't remove it.

'Contessa how delightful to see you. I trust you had a good flight?'

'Stephen, I have been traumatised—one of my vanity cases was misplaced. I was distraught—almost inconsolable.' She waved her hand at the throng. 'These kind gentlemen offered to help.' She dabbed her eye with a lace handkerchief. 'I feel so vulnerable—such an innocent in the ways of the modern world.'

Kelly smiled; he would have laughed but he didn't want to spoil her performance. Her audience stood transfixed and he had an urge to applaud her audacity.

'Thank you gentlemen,' he said, 'I shall see that the Contessa is taken care of.'

Once the crowd had dispersed she whispered, 'They wanted to search my case—let us leave before they change their minds.'

The three of them quickly pushed the trollies through the arrivals hall and out of the building. A large white 4x4 was parked outside. Dean got out of the driver's seat and helped them load the cases into the boot while Kelly opened the rear door for his guests. The Contessa climbed into the rear but her sister got into the passenger seat alongside Dean. Kelly sat next to the Contessa who seemed ill at ease in the vulgar interior.

'The Hilton,' said Kelly, tapping Dean on the shoulder.

'OK—Mr K.' Dean started the car.

They drove from the terminal past the large sculpture of the Beatle's *Yellow Submarine* and through Speke towards the city centre. Kelly, sitting in the rear with the Contessa, looked at his fellow passengers and idly gave them nicknames from *Alice in Wonderland:* Alice, the Red Queen and of course Tweedle-Dean but who was he? Then he realised—the Mad Hatter. He managed to stifle his laugh and received an icy glare from the Contessa who appeared to be in a particularly bad mood sitting in her red leather throne.

Eloise seemed fascinated by Dean. 'Are you really a *brother*?' she asked him after a few minutes.

'Wot?'

'One of *us*?'

Kelly interrupted. 'Yes he is, but only just—we can't *sense* him yet.'

She touched Dean's thigh: 'So, they call you Dean?'

'Me friends call me Deano—short fer Dean O'Reilly.'

'Dino?—You're Italian?'

'No, me mam an' dad ar' deffo Scousers.'

She laughed. 'You're so *funny*, Dino.'

Dean looked at Kelly and shrugged and Kelly laughed. The Contessa scowled.

It was a short drive into the city centre but there were road works and their arrival coincided with the Liverpool rush hour and soon they were stuck in traffic. Eloise chatted to Dean and the Contessa seemed preoccupied; Kelly was left alone with his thoughts.

The Contessa had looked so at home in Venice, sitting in *Florian's* sipping her cappuccino, her Dior sunglasses perched on her nose. But here—how strange she looked, as though she'd chosen a *look* many years before and hadn't changed with the times. Perhaps that was why she seemed so angry? Perhaps she'd realised that she was an alien here, not of this time or place. When she'd called herself 'an innocent in the ways of the modern world' he'd thought it a clever conceit to avoid customs but perhaps there was an element of truth to it after all.

When they'd met for lunch the day after they'd drugged him, she'd been so relaxed and friendly. She'd been dressed much as today but somehow it had seemed natural and not the affectation it now appeared. Her sister Eloise, if she was in fact her sister and not just a *sister*, also seemed a fish out of water. She dressed as if she were a child. Her past had not been fully explained and his subsequent research on the Foscari family had yielded many sisters but no others with a portrait that had survived.

That morning they'd met as arranged at *Florian's* and after a coffee, the sisters had taken him for lunch at *Harry's Bar* nearby. The Contessa had explained the bar's history and Kelly had played his tourist act to perfection, asked all the right questions: appeared to be surprised that this was where the Bellini cocktail had been created, and by all the famous people who had frequented the bar in the past. He neglected to mention that he'd been there before; he also failed to mention that he spoke passable Italian. He'd been particularly careful not to disclose that particular fact because he'd noticed that when the sisters wanted to keep something from him they would whisper to one another in Italian. So far he'd been able to gather that there was some other reason why they wanted to see Melville again—other than the reason that they'd given him—but precisely what that other reason was he still didn't know.

They'd sat at a round table in a small private room and the white-jacketed waiters had bowed and scrapped around the Contessa. They knew she was someone of importance even if they had no idea who she was; she had an air of entitlement that Kelly both envied and despised in equal measure. She'd called for the Maître d' as though he was a close personal friend and he'd arrived immediately even though it was obvious to Kelly that he didn't recognise her either. The man had obviously played this role before with other *celebrities* and he behaved as though she was a regular visitor. She'd ordered lunch without consulting the menu or the others. Within minutes a waiter returned with a silver tray and three Bellini cocktails. Kelly sipped his and it was as good as he remembered. The taste unlocked a distant memory, of an evening in 1949.

§

It was late evening; Harry's Bar was crowded and everyone was in good spirits. They'd had an excellent day's shooting on the lagoon and Kelly had a brace of mallard on the chair next to him. He felt pleased with himself; it always felt good to kill something, even a duck. His fellow hunters were drunk and had started singing. Kelly was, as always, sober, but he was pretending to be drunk.

He was observing his companions. They were a very mixed bag: a few dukes, some local dignitaries, two were from the U.S. Consulate and a large middle-aged American author who was fat, bearded and loud. Kelly had been told he was famous and was here to write a book, but he didn't recognise the man's name.

Eventually the singing faded and the revellers left one by one, until only Kelly and the author remained. The man called for grappa and insisted that Kelly joined him. Kelly accepted; he was alone in Venice and even vampires sometimes need company. They shared a bottle and some anecdotes. The author had been in the First World War—as had Kelly, although he was careful to attribute his knowledge of the conflict to recollections of his father. He looked too young to have taken part. The author told some tall stories of his hunting and fishing escapades and as the grappa flowed the stories grew taller, until, eventually, Kelly decided to outdo the author. He told him that he was over a hundred years old, had fought in the American Civil War and was a vampire. The author paused and studied Kelly face looking for any glimmer of a smile, then he laughed slapped him on the back.

'You're a lying son of a bitch,' he'd said, 'but you've the best poker face of anyone I've ever seen dead or alive.'

Kelly had laughed and poured them both another drink. By midnight the author was so drunk he could hardly stand up and Kelly decided to walk him back to his hotel, the Gritti Palace, carefully coaxing and cajoling him towards it. They were only a few yards away when the author took exception to something Kelly did or said and took a swing at him. Kelly, sober and much stronger, ducked then hit the man in the stomach; the man fell to the ground and was promptly sick on Kelly's shoe. Kelly wiped the vomit off his shoe onto the man's coat and contemplated throwing him in the canal but then he paused, he'd been an amusing companion after all, and he'd no desire to cut the man's throat and drink his blood—not when he was covered in vomit. He picked him up by the sleeve, dragged him to the door of the hotel and handed him over to the night porter who seemed accustomed to welcoming him back in that condition.

The porter winked at Kelly and said, 'Good morning, Mister Hemmingway,'

§

A car horn jolted Kelly back to the present where, after a long crawl through the traffic, they had at last reached the Hilton Hotel, opposite Albert Dock. The car park in front of the main entrance was full and as they got out of the car and unloaded the cases the doorman approached and asked them to move because they were blocking the entrance to the hotel. Kelly peeled a few notes from his money clip.

'Sorry friend, can you give us a minute or two? The keys are in the ignition if you need to move it.'

The doorman grumbled slightly but pocketed the money.

Once the Contessa and her sister were inside and had checked in, Kelly and Dean returned to the car and drove north towards Southport.

'So, Dean, what do you think of our guests?' Kelly asked.

'Well, Mr K, the young one is dead creepy—she really freaks me out. And the posh one's like me old teacher Miss Jones who always used to slap me legs when I wer a kid.'

Kelly laughed: 'As they say, "From the mouths of babes"…'

'Sorry, Mr K?'

'Nothing, Dean—just drive.'

They stopped at a set of traffic lights and Kelly could tell that Dean wanted to say something.

'OK, Dean—what is it?'

'Yer said that *we* don't get on? Like you an' Melville—like us vampires that is.'

'Correct, Dean.'

'So why 'ave you asked them two to stay, like?'

'You're not a stupid as you look—are you,' Kelly laughed.

'Thanks?' Dean scowled.

'It was a compliment—of sorts.' Kelly smiled. 'Let me tell you a story, Dean. Many, many years ago I was on a ship we'll call the '*Oreto*'. We were stuck in the Bahamas waiting for our armaments to arrive by another ship when the crew contracted yellow fever and many died. By the time we were able to set sail, the ship was infested with rats. We tried traps and poison to no avail, then one of the local sailors told me what to do.

I took a large barrel, sealed up the lid and made a trap door in the side, then I put some rotten meat inside and left the barrel in the hold. At first the door was screwed shut but the rats could smell the meat slowly decaying and were frantically trying to chew their way inside. I left it for two days then, on the third day, went down into the hold with a burning torch to scare away the rats and opened the door. The rats poured into the barrel from every nook and cranny in the ship, clambering over one another in their eagerness to get to the meat. I left them at it for a few hours then crept down into the hold and screwed the door shut.'

'Wot d'yer do then?'

'Nothing.'

'Nothin'—why?'

'First they ate the meat, then they fought and then they ate one another. It took three days until only one was left; it was half dead; it had lost an ear and part of its tail.'

'Wot d'yer do then?'

'Killed it.'

'Wot's that gorra do wiv them two?'

'Think of Liverpool as the barrel. We let those two meet Melville and Malone and stand well back. Whoever survives—we move in and deal with them while they're still weak. No more competition and we've got the city to ourselves again—do you understand?'

Dean nodded: 'That's dead sneaky Mr K.'

'And while they're busy we'll deal with a few loose ends of our own. That concierge and his girlfriend could still identify us; they need to be dealt with. I want you to find out where he lives; and keep an eye on Melville and Malone—they can't *sense* you yet—I want to know where they go.'

'No worries, Mr K.'

Kelly did worry, but he had no alternative. Dean was all he had and now that his guests had arrived he would definitely need someone to watch his back. A few minutes later they pulled up outside Kelly's apartment in Southport and Kelly got out.

'Pick me up here at ten tomorrow morning,' he said, '- then we'll go and see how the Red Queen and Alice are settling in.'

'Who?' asked Dean.

'Nothing—just be here at ten.'

§

The Contessa had eaten her breakfast and was now sitting in an armchair studying the apartment block on the other side of Chavasse Park through a pair of opera glasses. The glasses were covered in mother of pearl and she was holding them in one elegant hand, a coffee cup in the other.

'Which apartment did Stephen say was his?' she asked Eloise.

'Third floor from the top and three quarters of the way along.'

'Ah, I have it now. The blinds are raised but I can see no sign of life—or death.'

Eloise stood alongside her chair. 'Isn't there something moving in the end room?'

'Ah yes, I can see something now.'

A woman came to the window of the apartment with a mug in her hand and looked directly towards the Contessa. The magnification of the opera glasses made her seem much closer than she was and the Contessa was momentarily taken aback and even assumed that she'd been seen, then the woman looked away and the Contessa realised that she hadn't. The woman had her hair in large curlers and was wearing a bright pink track suit.

'So this is her—the Malone woman.' The Contessa passed the opera glasses to her sister and took a sip of cappuccino. 'You can see what she is ... cheap trash.'

'Is that him behind her?'

The Contessa snatched back the opera glasses. A tall dark-haired man appeared alongside the woman and put his arm around her shoulder. The woman took a sip from her mug and when she turned and looked up at him she had a large foam moustache. The Contessa could see them laughing.

'Laugh now Richard Melville you and your little tart—soon you shall have tears.'

She passed the opera glasses to her sister who studied them for a few moments then asked: 'What do we do about Stephen?'

'What do they say—"Too many cooks"?' The Contessa smiled. 'Once we have dealt with the Malone woman we shall have to decide who to keep—Stephen or Richard.'

'What about Dino?'

The Contessa laughed: 'An amusing idea—but no.'

Her sister huffed and folded her arms: 'Why can't I ever have anyone?'

'Enjoy him while you can; you are too young to have a companion—or even a pet.'

'Why do I always have to be the younger sister or the servant?'

'Because you look younger; I was your servant once.'

'When?'

'In Vienna.'

'When?'

'The first time—you were a princess and I was your governess. Am I not correct?'

Eloise huffed and sat down heavily on the sofa. 'Why can't I be a princess now?'

'In Liverpool?'

'But you're a Contessa.'

'Exactly, let that be an end to it—perhaps next time.'

The phone on the bedside table rang and Eloise answered it.

'Stephen and Dino are here; I said to send them up.'

'Excellent—call room service and order coffee for our guests.'

An hour later the coffee had been drunk and a plan of campaign had been agreed; Kelly and Dean had left once more. The two women sat side by side staring at Melville's apartment which now appeared to be empty. The Contessa placed her half empty cup on the table between them.

'They called *that* an americano?—disgusting.'

'Would you like something else?' asked Eloise.

The Contessa shook her head. 'To business.'

'How shall we start this time?'

'As always sister, slowly. You go with Dino as agreed, find out all you can about our friend Stephen. I do not trust him -' the Contessa smiled '- we are too alike.'

'And what will you do?'

'I shall arrange a tearful reconciliation with my long lost love.'

'Why can't I meet him too?'

'You are too impetuous my dear. You shall meet him soon enough but I shall occupy him while you deal with his little tart.'

'How?'

I'm sure you can remember *how*—it is the where and when that we need to decide.'

Dean drove up to the front of the Hilton again. He wasn't sure what he was doing there. It had been agreed earlier that morning that he'd give the creepy younger one a guided tour of Liverpool. He wasn't keen, but he hadn't been consulted. All Kelly had said was to not to say too much and to try and find out anything he could about the sisters. As far as Dean was concerned he didn't have much to say anyway; he'd been hired by Kelly as 'scum' and been told not to ask questions, just do what he was told, and that's what he intended to do now. He still wasn't sure about all this vampire stuff. OK, so he didn't die when that fat bastard shot him and he'd come over all 'Incredible Hulk' when Moxy and his boys tried to rough him up—but that might be the drugs they pumped him full of in the hospital. He checked his teeth in the rear view mirror—still not pointy. Kelly was full of shit.

The doorman tapped on the car window.

'Yer can't park 'ere—shift it.'

Dean was about to give him a mouthful when the girl ran up to the car and jumped into the passenger seat. He gave the doorman a one-fingered salute and drove off at speed.

The tour was not a success. She was less impressed that he'd expected by the football stadium and, apparently, she'd seen bigger and better cathedrals elsewhere. Now it was late afternoon and they were parked on the promenade next to Festival Park overlooking the Mersey. Dean fiddled with the radio looking for some dance music and Eloise stretched out in the passenger seat. She was playing with her hair.

'Do you think I'm pretty Dino?'

'S'pose.' Dean didn't look up.

'Do you have a wife?'

'Wot?!'

'Girlfriend?'

Dean continued to fiddle with the car stereo.

'It's shit hot this sound system—500 watts. It'll make yer ears bleed.'

'This is good?' Eloise was confused.

'Too fuckin' right!'

Suddenly the radio came on incredibly loudly, Eloise reached over and turned down the volume.

'Do you have anything quieter—more romantic?'

'Cud be summin' in ther?' Dean shrugged and pointed to the glove box.

There was only one CD, a Christmas compilation so they sat by the Mersey while the stereo blasted out an Eighties classic and Eloise sang along,

'Last Christmas I gave you my heart, but the very next day, you gave it away …'

'Wot d'yer wanna do now?' Dean asked sulkily.

She turned down the stereo and put her hand on his thigh. 'I'm sure you can think of something, Dino.'

'Ang on jailbait—keep yer 'ands to yerself!'

'You're so funny,' she laughed. 'This is your Liverpool sense of humour—no?'

'Yer too fuckin' young!'

'You have no idea how old I am—don't be silly.'

'I can use me eyes. I'm not a fuckin' kiddy fiddler; back off!'

They sat in awkward silence for a few minutes then Eloise pouted and asked.

'Teach me to drive, Dino.'

He reluctantly agreed—anything to keep her hands occupied—it was mid-week and the road was deserted. He folded up his coat to raise her up sufficiently to see over the bonnet and, the car being an automatic, he soon had her driving backwards and forward along the promenade. She'd driven many times before but didn't mention it because she wanted an opportunity to practice driving this particular car. It might come in useful once they'd dealt with the competition.

'Yer a fuckin' natural girl.'

'You're a good teacher, Dino.' She smiled. 'What are you going to teach me now?'

She raised an eyebrow and reached towards him and he leapt in his seat. She laughed.

After dropping her back at the Hilton, he drove to the industrial unit as instructed. He hated going there. It gave him the creeps; he felt that it must be haunted by the people Kelly had killed and tortured there. He knew that Lewis had been freaked out by it too. He thought about his brother, wondered how he'd really died, wondered how she'd killed him. He parked in front of the unit and was about to switch off the engine.

'Cut me throat Dean …'ere to 'ere.'

Dean swore. He turned slowly and Lewis was sitting in the passenger seat.

'Then she drank me blood.'

Dean leapt out of the car and ran into the unit where Kelly was waiting for him.

'What's the matter, Dean,' Kelly laughed. '- did Eloise try to take a bite out of you?'

They sat in the office and Kelly made Dean explained slowly and in detail exactly what had happened and what had been said during the tour—twice.

'That all? Then you gave her a driving lesson?'

'Yeah.'

'Nothing more about Melville?'

'Nah, just 'er sister knew 'im yonks ago in Belgium.'

'Did Eloise know him too?'

'Nah, she wudda been a sprog.

'Sprog?'

'Baby—yer know, if it wer yonks ago, like.'

'She's older than she looks, Dean'

'Yer can't fool me, Mr K. Wot is she thirteen—fourteen?'

'Could be five hundred for all I know.'

'Don't take the piss, Mr K. D'yer think 'im sum sorra divy?'

Kelly sat back in his chair and put his feet on the desk.

'I wonder how the Red Queen got on with Melville?' he said.

§

That evening the sisters sat in the hotel restaurant deep in conversation. The pasta had been acceptable, the wine good and the Bellinis were excellent. The Contessa's mood had improved considerably.

'Richard was so surprised to see me. I thought he was going to cry—it was quite touching.'

'Did you meet her too—the tart?'

'I was careful to catch him alone. It is for the best that she has no idea that we are here—until it is too late.'

'What if he tells her?'

'He will not. I understand men. He will be cautious—they are such cowards.'

'What next?'

'We have agreed to meet again tomorrow—discretely.'

'Why can't I have a cocktail?' Eloise pouted.

'You know full well sister—play your role!'

Eloise huffed and sipped orange juice through a straw.

'Stephen thinks I'm old enough,' she said.

'It is obvious what Stephen thinks you are old enough *for*, sister—and it is not cocktails. With luck we may be able to use his *weakness* to our advantage. We have done much the same before, have we not?'

Eloise made a loud noise as she sucked up the last of her drink.

'What of Dean?' asked the Contessa.

'He's only been with Stephen for a few weeks. I don't think he realises that he's *family* yet. Thinks he was just lucky to survive being shot. Did you know his brother was killed by the tart?'

'Interesting. What does he know about Stephen?'

'Nothing, thinks he's drug dealer.'

The Contessa laughed: 'Really?'

'Really.'

'That calls for a celebration. Waiter—another Bellini—and an orange juice for my sister.'

10am the following day, Melville was taking his usual morning walk and made a slight detour to collect the Contessa as arranged. He still didn't understand why he hadn't mentioned to Sheryl that he'd met her the previous day. It was probably because, when she'd asked him, he'd still been slightly disorientated after a surprise meeting with an ex-lovers after two centuries. He knew what she'd have said anyway: 'Why would he want to have anything to do with a heartless cow like Isabella?' In fact, if anyone had asked him the day before, that's exactly what he would have said himself. However, when he'd met her all those thoughts had disappeared in an instant. All he could remember was how much he'd loved her.

He'd planned to tell Sheryl about the meeting last night but now there was no need; Sheryl had stormed off before he'd had a chance, although he still didn't understand why—they hadn't even had an argument. Well he'd just meet her as arranged and then tell Sheryl afterwards once she'd calmed down. He walked into the foyer and the Contessa stood up to embrace him.

'My dearest Major Melville. I have dreamed of this day for so long."

'Lieutenant.'

'Are you sure?—I am seldom wrong.'

'Yes.'

'What of it. Social standing is so unimportant to a true love, my dearest Richard.'

'It's Lee now.'

'Why not Richard? It is such a noble name. Lee is so...'

'I prefer Lee.'

'I can see you have much to tell me; let us walk and talk.'

They walked across the Strand into Albert Dock arm in arm and Melville gave a brief summary of his last two hundred years. She asked many questions but said little herself.

'How long have you been in this city, Richar- Lee?'

'A few months. You?'

'Days. Are there others of our kind here?'

'My girlfriend and –'

'A girlfriend? I must meet her; I know we shall be great friends. Where is she?'

'Erm, she's gone away for a few days.'

'Looking for fresh blood?'

'Yes.'

He had no intention of introducing either women to one another if he could avoid it. Something told him that it was highly unlikely that they would be *great friends*. In fact, he'd be willing to bet on the opposite and he had no desire to be in the middle of the subsequent bloodbath.

That afternoon the Contessa sat in the Hotel bar with Eloise.

'The tart is called Sheryl Malone,' she said. 'Such a common name, he even had an old photograph of her in his wallet. He says that she is away for a few days -but he is such a bad liar.'

Eloise sat on a bar stool, playing with the straw in her orange juice and watching the young barman as he made another Bellini for her sister, trying to decide which she coveted the most.

'I have talked to Stephen,' the Contessa continued. 'Dean has been watching them for the last few days and will contact us when the tart is alone. We have agreed that you will deal with her because she would recognise him and I will be occupied with Richard.'

'How?'

'You will need a disguise. It is important that you blend in.'

'And money?'

'Take one of my cards.'

An hour later Eloise was in Liverpool city centre. She'd looked in a few shop windows and was now thoroughly confused as to what a local would wear. She was out of touch and had worn the same style for many years as had her sister. A fifth person had just asked her where her white rabbit was and she decided that she was somehow conspicuous. Two young girls walked towards her deep in conversation. One was wearing the same pink tracksuit that she'd seen Melville's tart wearing through the opera glasses. Both girls had their hair in large rollers.

'Excuse me,' she said.

'Hiya Babe- where's yer white rabbit?' Both laughed.

'Sorry?'

'What's with the *Disney* characters get-up, luv? D'yer pay a quid to 'ave a selfie took with yer?'

'Selfie? I don't understand. I want clothes like yours—where do I go?'

'No worries, babe.' They took an arm each and guided her down the street. 'Yer wanna be a Liver bird?—cum wiv us.'

A few hours later she returned to the hotel. It was difficult to walk in the high heels so she changed into her old shoes until she was outside their room then changed back before the Contessa saw her. The artificial nails made it hard to use the door key but eventually she stumbled inside and dumped her carrier bags on the floor by the door.

'Ciao,' she said.

'Ciao,'— the Contessa was reading a local newspaper—'such a strange city they keep their statues under water. Look here; they call it—*Another Place*—a hundred iron men on a beach!'

Eloise put her hands on her hips and struck a theatrical pose.

'Tah dah! Do you like the disguise?'

The Contessa looked up from the newspaper.

'Mother of God!' she said. 'What has happened to you? Why are you *orange*?'

'Bermuda glow it's called. Everyone wears it.'

'That dress—why is it so short? What has happened to your bosoms?'

'Chicken fillets.'

'Chicken *what*?'

'You like it?' Eloise did a twirl.

'Sister, how can I put this? You look—perfect.'

Eloise kicked off the high heels and slumped into an armchair. 'What now?' she asked.

'Dean will follow the tart tonight and call us when she is alone.' She patted Eloise on the knee. 'You shall do the rest.'

'What then?'

'Stephen wants us to abduct her. He no doubt has his own plans for her, but we should take no risks—we do not want them forming an alliance against us. If we get the opportunity we should dispose of her once and for all.'

'What about Stephen and Dino?'

'Likewise.'

'You intend to keep Richard then?'

'Perhaps ... providing he remains useful—and amusing. We are playing a difficult game sister: imagine a Chess board with no black or white pieces, only grey. Who is friend? Who is foe? One cannot tell, everyone is a threat. Stephen wants us to be his pawns, but we must make sure that he is ours.'

'How?'

'I've arranged to meet Richard this evening to keep him occupied. Dean will accompany you to a rendezvous with the tart and, if you feel that there is an opportunity to deal with her tonight, contact me immediately. Once we have disposed of her then we can decide who to side with: Richard or Stephen.'

§

Sheryl leaned on the bar and whistled the barman.

'The usual?' he asked, 'Liver Bird with cherries?'

'Ahh, you remember, hun?'

'How could I forget?'

She sat back on the bar stool and surveyed the room. 'Just like old times,' she thought.

The cocktail arrived with three cherries; she laughed and winked at the barman. Lee was so boring; he never wanted to come out hunting. That was the problem with being a couple, you couldn't do your own thing. Well, now she was free to do whatever she wanted without having to worry about Lee and his guilty conscience. Perhaps it was time to move on, find a new territory and more 'hot dates'. It wasn't as if she had any reason to stay in Liverpool. Her sister was dead and Lathom would look after Michelle and Natasha.

She sipped her cocktail. Why hadn't he come to see her at Lathom's? He must be feeling too guilty. She'd let him sweat, wait until he was begging her to return. But what if he didn't want her back? What if it was this other woman he went to see every day when he went for his walk? Had he been lying to her from the very beginning?

The bar was getting busier. She turned on her stool, looking for a suitable 'hot date' and suddenly she sensed another vampire in the room and turned around on the stool to look in the mirror behind the bar, hoping it was Lee but also dreading that it might be Kelly. She could see no one she recognised.

'Ciao.'

A small woman appeared next to her.

'Jesus!—you made me jump,' said Sheryl.

The woman giggled. 'Don't worry, sister—I won't bite.'

Sheryl laughed and held out her hand: 'Sheryl, Sheryl Malone.'

'Eloise.'

'Can I get yer a cocktail, babe?' Sheryl decided to use her Scouse accent until she had the measure of this unknown woman. She didn't want to give too much away; such encounters were always unpredictable.

'Gracia, sister, a Bellini.'

Sheryl caught the barman's eye.

'Same again, hun, and a Bellini fer me mate 'ere.'

The two women took their drinks to a secluded table.

'Well, babe, yer passin' thru' or plannin' on stoppin'?'

'Just a brief visit, sister; you need have no concern. We're no threat to you.'

'We?'

'My sister and I.'

'She 'ere too?' Sheryl looked around the room.

'At our hotel but she'd love to meet you—we could go now.' Eloise looked over the top of her glass and nodded at a drunk young woman at the next table. 'Perhaps we could all share something later?'

Sheryl followed her eyes and smiled. 'Yer, that cud be a laugh, babe.'

They walked down Seel Street towards the Hilton Hotel, a large white 4X4 was parked by the side of the road, its hazard warning lights flashing.

'Eloise that's dead pretty. Did it used to be Elsie?'

'When?'

'Before, when yer wer' *made*? I wuz Shirley first; now it's Sheryl.'

'Yes, I think I've been Elsie—once. So many names, Esmeralda, Estella, Emma.'

'Emma?'

'Yes.' She pointed towards the car. 'Here's my sister now.'

A blonde woman in a red dress was standing beside the 4X4. Eloise pulled out a large orange pen from her handbag as they walked towards the car.

'You were an *Emma* once?' Sheryl took Eloise by the arm. 'When?'

'Long ago?'

'Stupid tart,' said the woman in the red dress.

'What did you just say?' asked Sheryl scowling at her,

'She *was* Emma … I *was* Isabella.'

'Oww!' Sheryl looked back at Eloise. 'What was that?'

'…And you *are* dead.'

5

ANOTHER PLACE

They carried Sheryl's unconscious body to the 4X4 and dumped it on the back seat. At this time of the evening any passer-by would probably think that she was drunk. The Contessa got in alongside her and Eloise sat in the passenger's seat next to Dean. The Contessa tapped Dean on the shoulder.

'Take us to the industrial unit.'

'But? I thought that –'

'There has been a change of plan—drive!'

Dean grumbled but obeyed. Fifteen minutes later they pulled up outside Kelly's unit. Dean unlocked the steel shutters then pressed a button at the side and the door gradually rolled upwards.

'Once inside we kill them both,' the Contessa whispered to Eloise, 'then we take the car back to the hotel. I have arranged to meet Richard tomorrow morning and we shall decide then whether to side with him or Stephen.'

'You think we should side with one of them?'

'For the time being. It will be advantageous to have someone with local knowledge—at first.'

'Why kill the girl?'

'I despise her; Richard appears besotted, and have you heard how Stephen talks about her? I shall have no competition from a tart like her.'

'Can I keep Dino then?'

'No.'

Eloise pulled a face like a spoilt child. 'At least let me play with them.'

'If you must, but only for a short time. Your last *playtime* was excessive. How can it take three days to kill someone?'

'It takes a long time to skin someone—completely.'

'As long as they are both dead by tomorrow morning.'

Dean walked back to the car, drove it into the unit then carried Sheryl into the shower room. He dumped her unconscious body on the tiled floor then handcuffed her hands behind her back and tied her ankles together with a piece of rope.

'Now take us back to the hotel,' said the Contessa.

'No way! Mr K sed to stay wiv 'er.'

'Then give me the car keys.' She held out her hand.

'But-'

The Contessa fixed him with a steely glare; Dean grumbled and handed her the keys.

'Don't worry, Dino,' Eloise giggled. 'I'll stay and keep you company.'

'I shall collect *you* in the morning,' said the Contessa.

Eloise smiled.

The Contessa started the car and reversed out. Dean pressed the button on the inside of the door and the shutter rolled closed.

Eloise sat on the long metal work bench that stretched the length of the back wall swinging her legs, there was a ghetto blaster next to her. 'Play me some music Dino,' she said.

'Got nothin' to play.'

'What else can we do?' She stretched out on the bench and toyed with her hair.

'There's sum cards in the office.'

She sat up and laughed. 'You're so funny Dino.' She reached into her handbag and held up a CD.

'Play my favourite song, Dino.'

He put the CD in the player and pressed play. *Last Christmas I gave you my heart ...*

'Dunno why yer like this one—its shite.' He picked up the orange epi-pen, 'How does this work?'

Eloise snatched it from him. 'Look, it holds five doses. You twist this and it primes it, then all you do is—press.'

'Oww! What the fuc-?' Dean fell to the floor. Eloise stood over him smiling, then took a curved knife from her handbag.

§

Natasha had caught the next train into Liverpool and was now in Kelly's apartment in Rumford Court. It was later than she wanted it to be; she needed to get the last train north to her mum's flat otherwise she'd either have to get a taxi, which would be expensive, or go back to Peter's apartment in Cheapside and explain where she'd been all evening. She'd managed to download Kelly's files onto the *Mickey Mouse* memory stick and was now sorting through the random collection of items in the tin: buttons; a silver brooch in the shape of a butterfly, wristwatch, comb, and the label from the IKEA rug. Why did Kelly have the label off an identical rug to the one Peter had in his apartment? Or could it be that this was the one off Peter's rug? She took the label and tucked it in her purse; she'd see if it matched next time she was alone in the apartment. Was it possible that Peter had known Kelly beforehand and that her abduction was nothing to do with the government? She'd check the label before she asked any difficult questions. She had no idea about Peter's past life or if he'd only just met Kelly, Lee and Sheryl as he'd told her—or if they had known one another for much longer. There were inconsistencies in the story he'd told her. Why had he gone to their apartment that night when Kelly had expressly told him not too? Peter had never explained that adequately. He'd told her that he was confused and had panicked and gone to the only people who could explain what was happening, the people whom the package was addressed to. Why hadn't he gone to the police? That would have made more sense, unless he was somehow involved in something criminal, but she found that hard to believe. Peter was so honest he'd even tell the waitress if she'd undercharged him. But you heard about scientists being blackmailed to make drugs for criminals; perhaps that was it and they were all in drug cartel: she'd been kidnapped to keep Peter from going to the police. But if so, where did that leave her new Granddad, Bob? Was he a victim or a villain? Natasha checked her watch and snatched the memory stick from the computer; she'd just have time to make the train if she ran. She needed to give it all some serious thought. At the moment it was too confusing, there were too many seemingly random bits of information: Kelly's list on his computer, the label from the rug; not to mention, Bob, Sheryl and Lee. It was like a puzzle, but one where you didn't understand the rules. Once she understood what it was all about then perhaps everything would all slot into place. Part of her wanted to go and confront Peter now, but he'd probably only evade her questions. It would be better to wait until tomorrow. She ran towards Moorgate Station and caught the last train as it was about to leave, with luck she'd be back at her mum's flat before her mum returned from Maggie's; then no one would know she'd been out tonight.

§

Kelly was sitting on a bench in St Nicholas's Churchyard when he received the message from Dean. They'd got Sheryl Malone and he was taking her to the industrial unit as agreed. The Contessa had already arranged to meet Melville the following morning and Kelly would accompany her. He was looking forward to seeing Melville's face when he turned up. Kelly decided to return to his old flat at Rumford Court; he hadn't been there since the Mexican stand-off with Malone and the red-headed girl, he'd thought it too risky until now.

He walked the short distance from the Churchyard deep in thought. Once Melville and Malone were out of the way, he'd get rid of their family and friends as well because he didn't want any witnesses. After that, all he had to decide was what to do about the Contessa and Eloise, whether to keep either of them or neither. Three would definitely be a crowd, four if you counted Dean—not that he ever did. He was very aware that they were no doubt making plans about him too, so he needed to make an alliance with one of them soon, or quickly dispose of them both. He still didn't fully understand what had happened in the past between them and Melville; the Contessa had been careful not to give away too many details. Perhaps they were using him to get rid of Malone and, if that was the case, no doubt he would be next on the list. He needed to keep his head and watch for any attempts to double-cross him. Melville and the Malone put on a good act of being in love but he knew it was an act; a vampire didn't need love—all you needed was blood.

He was about to cross the road and walk back to his apartment in Rumford Place but he still felt restless. The night was yet young and perhaps he could find a 'soft centre' to amuse him and take his mind off tomorrow's decisions. He turned right and walked along Tithebarn Street away from the river. The streets were deserted and as he walked he thought about what he would do with Melville. He'd waited so long for this moment and he'd been so close twice before this year, yet on both occasions he'd come off worse. He'd lost an eye and a hand the first time; the second he'd been driven from the city. But he was back now and revenge would soon be his. He hadn't talked to Melville since that night in the Churchyard over a hundred and fifty years ago but he understood him. They were kindred spirits—blood brothers. Kelly smiled to himself, perhaps he should just make a deal with Melville to share the city and they could then dispose of all the others? After all this whole idea of revenge had more to do with relieving the boredom of eternal life than with any real grievance. That was why vampires thought up more and more extreme ways of killing or torturing their victims. It was from their need for excitement, for novelty. Forever often seemed a very long time indeed.

He had walked nearly to the end of Tithebarn Street and was considering turning around and heading home — there seemed no further opportunity for amusement tonight—when he read the name of the side road, 'Cheapside', and it jogged his memory. He checked his wallet and there were the addresses that Dean had found out for him. Perhaps he could kill two birds with one stone; and enjoy a little light relief from his current worries? He walked down Cheapside until he reached a new apartment block that somehow looked familiar, although there were so many springing up all over the city that it was unlikely. He checked the address then pressed the intercom button for the apartment on his list. A voice answered.

'Hello?'

'Hello, I'm sorry it's so late sir. P C Makintosh here, Merseyside Police. I've some bad news for you. Do you mind if I come up?'

The intercom buzzed and the door opened. Kelly smiled and entered.

§

Lathom collected his car from the resident's car park and headed north out of the city. He turned off the Dock Road and drove slowly passed a scruffy pub. It was too late for it to be open and before parking he went once around the block and then, to be certain, tried the roads on the other side of the Dock Road, it was then that he spotted the Jaguar. It was tucked in a dead end, off a small side road, not visible from the main road.

'Good—but not good enough,' thought Lathom. He parked next to the Jaguar and checked the driver's door, which was open. He searched the car and found the keys under the driver's seat as he'd expected and put them in his pocket. There was no way this man was getting away.

He drove his car back to the pub and parked a little way up the road. He assumed his target was already within. He had the advantage of surprise: the man in the Jaguar would no doubt expect Lathom to have been killed by the car bomb, but Danny was probably still at risk until they knew he was dead.

Lathom gently pushed at the pub door, a 'Chow Mein' special in one pocket and Flanagan's Browning in the other. The door was locked so he went around the back and, after clambering over the pile of empty crates, tried the back door which opened—he crept inside. Music came from the direction of the bar. He took the 'Chow Mein' special from his pocket and screwed on its silencer, moving silently through the small kitchen and hallway until only a swing door separated him from the bar. He paused, took a deep breath and slowly opened the door with his left hand, the gun in his right.

It was dark inside the bar, illuminated only by the street light outside; the juke-box blared out a 60's tune. The man with his back to him was wearing a waxed jacket and a flat cap and was splashing petrol from a red ready-can onto the furniture and curtains. Lathom slowly walked into the bar and saw Danny's body on the floor next to the counter. He'd been shot in the head at close range, the bullet hole a small red circle in the middle of his forehead with a large exit wound in the back of his head. A pool a blood surrounded him like a crimson halo.

Lathom pulled back the hammer on the gun, with the click the man spun around, the petrol can still in his hands.

'Hello, John, been busy I see,' said Lathom.

The man glanced to where his gun lay on the top of a table by the door.

'Don't try it—OK?' Lathom moved over to the table and picked up the gun, a service-issue Browning, identical to Flanagan's gun in his other pocket. He kept the man covered and a safe distance between them. He indicated Danny's body.

'Why?' he asked.

'Why not—just clearing up loose ends. You know the score, Bob.'

'The Old man send you—or the Department?'

'You expect me to tell you?'

'Yes—unless you want to be the one getting the flowers.'

'You'll kill me anyway.'

'Why should I? You tell the Old Man that the bomb didn't go off and I'll disappear. I don't want my family involved—OK?'

'OK—for old time's sake. It was the Old Man, got too much to lose if it all comes out.' John laughed. 'Doesn't want to lose his chance of a peerage, does he?'

'Take off your coat and hat, and turn around.'

'Why?'

'I want to search you.'

The man did as he was told then turned his back on Lathom who shot him in the back of the head with his own gun. The man fell to the floor next to Danny.

'For old time's sake,' said Lathom.

He took off his coat with his passport in the pocket and

the plane tickets and hung it on the back of the chair next to the body. He swapped watches with the man, and then dowsed the body with petrol. Lathom put on the man's coat and hat, took a lighter from behind the bar and, after setting fire to one of the curtains, left by the back door. He walked quickly to his own car and put the car keys under the driver's seat then walked on to the Jaguar and started it with John's keys.

He was just entering the Mersey Tunnel when he heard the fire-engines.

§

Sheryl was gradually regaining consciousness. She tried to stretch out and realised that she was handcuffed behind her back and that her feet were tied together. As her vision cleared, she looked around the room. She seemed to be in some sort of communal shower room. The far wall had a Health-and-Safety notice, a fire alarm and a large red fire axe. It must be a factory. But where? How could she contact Lee to warn him? She was lying on a cold tiled floor next to a floor drain. The tiles were cracked and filthy and stained water had collected around the drain. It smelled of damp and decay. A few feet away from her was a large ceramic bath. She twisted around and got up onto her knees and peered over the edge. The bath was two thirds full of a cloudy liquid; a thick scum had formed around the edge and pungent fumes made her eyes water.

The door burst open and Eloise walked in singing and holding something in her bloody hands.

'Last Christmas I gave you my heart … The very next day you gave it away…'

She threw the object into the bath and it began to fizz, then wiped her hands on a rag and threw it on the floor.

'Good, I'm glad you've woken up. I've run out of people to play with.'

She walked back out of the room and returned with a chair; Sheryl's handbag and the ghetto blaster. She placed the chair next to Sheryl and began to sort through her handbag.

'So much make-up: mascara, eyebrow pencil, lipsticks. My sister won't let me wear make-up, she likes me to look young. You see she only wants the men looking at her—that's why she hates you.'

'Why?'

'You were the perfect age when you were *made*. That's why we both hate you. I was too young. I'll never grow up; I'll always be on the outside watching the grown-ups play—never be in my prime—never be lusted after by men—only by perverts.'

'What about your sister?'

'The opposite. She was once a great beauty, the Doge's favourite. She married well but produced no children; her husband was more interested in the young men of Venice than his trophy wife. Her looks had begun to wane and there were other younger favourites at court and she was aware that all eyes no longer turned to her when she entered a room. That was when she became one of *us*. She sees you as a threat that must be removed.'

Eloise took out a mirror and a lipstick. She carefully applied the lipstick and then checked the effect in the mirror from several angles.

'What do you think—perhaps a bit tarty?'

'Are you trying to get revenge on Lee?' Sheryl asked.

'Lee?—Oh, Lieutenant Melville. Why would I want revenge on him?'

'Because he killed you? Made you one of us?'

'Is that what he thinks?—Still? Hasn't he worked it out yet?' Eloise laughed.

'Worked what out?'

'He didn't kill me; I was already dead. It was because he was new that he couldn't sense that I was a vampire too. Isabella had planned it all in advance. We needed someone to kill her husband because he'd out grown his usefulness and we were bored in Brussels. It was time to move on but we needed money and a protector. In those days, two women travelling alone was suspicious so we needed a companion or, more accurately, a servant. She knew that she could twist Melville around her little finger but the timing had to be right and he was called to war early so she had to make sure he survived. That was why she made him one of us. However, by the time he came back she'd found a better alternative, a Russian Prince with money and plenty of servants. Now she only needed someone to get rid of her husband without any suspicion attaching itself to her or her prince. Melville was perfect, but we were concerned that his conscience would get the better of him. That's why I was there too. I had a knife and would do the killing if necessary, then blame it on him. No one ever suspects the little maid.

But he surprised us both; he killed the husband and then me. After he'd stabbed me he was so upset that I almost laughed out loud. He was so pathetic, crying and trying to revive me. Then he smelled the blood and I knew that we had him. Actually when he was drinking my blood it was quite an arousing experience.'

'So why are you doing this?'

'Doing what?'

'Why have you drugged me and brought me here.'

'To torture and then kill you. Then we'll do the same to the dear dolt Melville.'

'Why not just kill us?'

'That would be so boring. Surely you have some fun with yours too?'

'No.'

'How very dull. How long ago were you *made*?'

'Fifty years.'

'Wait until that's two hundred, then you'll appreciate the boredom. I'd give you some tips but you won't have a chance to use them—so I'll give you some first-hand experience instead.'

Eloise picked up a curved knife, its black blade inlaid with a silver design, and knelt beside Sheryl. She took hold of Sheryl's head by the hair and held the blade against her cheek.

'An Ottoman Khanjar– prefect for skinning.'

'No worries, babe, when I need a chemical peel I'll see the beautician not a teenage with acne and attitude.'

'You'll be laughing the other side of your face later—if you still have a face.' Eloise dragged Sheryl towards the bath by her hair.

'Watch out for me extensions, babe.'

Pushing Sheryl face first over the edge of the bath, Eloise explained: 'Nitric Acid, dissolves skin and bone—slowly.'

The fumes were hurting Sheryl's eyes and making tears run down her cheeks. She was glad she'd worn her waterproof mascara because she wanted to look her best as a corpse. Then, on the far side of the bath, she saw a human heart that was slowly dissolving. She was suddenly very frightened. She needed to think and decided to play for time.

'Whose is the heart?'

Eloise let go of Sheryl's hair.

'Dino was his name. I asked him to be my boyfriend—but he thought I was too young. My sister says that all men are stupid.'

How did you and your sister join the club?'

'You're almost as stupid as Melville; she's not my sister, just a *sister*. We're all brothers and sisters.'

'Did she *make* you then?'

'No,' Eloise laughed, '- we met over a body.'

Eloise sat on the chair and began sorting through Sheryl's handbag; Sheryl shuffled on her knees away from the bath of acid and towards her. Eloise pulled out Sheryl's phone, opened the case—then laughed.

'So many messages from that dear dolt Melville. "I love you"—"I miss you"—"I'm so sorry" … "Call me?"'

Eloise stood up and took a photo of Sheryl with the phone then sat down again. She typed a message.

'I'll just send him something to think about.'

'How were you *made* then—if Lee didn't do it?'

'Sorry?' Eloise looked up from the phone, then put it back in the bag without switching it off.

'How were you made?'

'It was during the French Revolution. I was working on the Guillotine clearing away the bodies and heads, bloody work but profitable. There were always opportunities to rob the dead of their fine clothes and valuables. I'd been in the Bastille awaiting execution for killing a client when it was stormed by the mob and I was set free. It seemed only polite to help with the clearing up and it was amusing to see the upper classes suffer for a change.

'Killing a client?'

'My parents sold me to a whorehouse in Paris where the rich clientele had an appetite for young girls. One day after about six months I got bored with pretending to be a virgin for the tenth time that day and decided to escape. I hid a long hat-pin under my pillow and when my latest client, a loathsome aristocrat named Du Pont, was asleep, I forced it between the vertebrae in his neck and severed his spinal cord. I ran away but I didn't get far. The authorities decided to make an example of me.'

'Weren't you too young to be executed, even then?'

'Yes, but the whorehouse had listed me as a maid and had documents with a false date of birth.'

'So how were you made?'

Eloise laughed. 'The truth is, I don't know. One of those executed must have been one of us; I must have just got blood in a cut. It was rough work. I didn't know what had happened until I met Isabella.'

'Why was she there?'

'She'd been mistress to some aristocrat and came to see him before he was executed. All crocodile tears of course, she only wanted to make sure that he didn't have any more valuables hidden away. She lost interest as soon as she realised he was penniless.'

'What happened then?' Sheryl was desperately playing for time her mind working overtime for a way to escape. She decided to take stock of the situation. She had her trusty penknife in her bra so they obviously hadn't searched her very thoroughly. She could use it to cut the rope around her ankles and defend herself if she could get her hands free—except they were handcuffed behind her back and she didn't know where the key was. She needed time and some way to distract the girl until she found a way to do this.

'Sorry?' Eloise was preoccupied sorting through Sheryl make-up.

'What happened then?'

'Oh, she *sensed* me. I felt something too but didn't know what it was. I thought it was more a sexual thing but then she explained what had happened to me and asked me to go with her. She had money from her aristocrat and we could travel as sisters or as a lady and her maid. I wanted to move on anyway and it seemed exciting. We've stayed together ever since.'

'What about her—when was she made?'

'Look, I know you're playing for time but Prince Charming isn't on his way. Let's get on—all this reminiscing is boring me.'

'Please, I'd like to know it all.'

Eloise looked at her watch.

'I'll give you a few minutes more. She's never told me everything but as far as I understand she was abducted by some Turk in the 15th Century. It took her nearly two hundred years to catch up with him.'

'What happened then?'

'She boiled him.'

'Boiled?'

'In a big pot. She needed a big pot; he was so fat. She says he squealed like a pig and when she tipped him out he was covered in large red blisters. She pricked them and peeled him like a tomato.'

'That wouldn't kill him.'

'No—she wanted him to suffer not die. When she grew bored with his whimpering she cut out his heart.' Eloise picked up the curved knife and knelt beside Sheryl, 'I'll do the same when I get bored with you, but that won't be for a long time. Shall we get started?'

Eloise looked at her watch. She switched on the ghetto blaster to drown out the screams, and began to drag Sheryl by her hair towards the bath of acid once again. Suddenly she paused and switched off the music.

'What was that noise?'

§

Melville heard his phone bleep with an incoming message. It was from Sheryl; perhaps now he'd find out where she was. He opened it. It was a photo of Sheryl handcuffed laying on a tiled floor. The caption read: 'Can't talk at the moment—too tied up.'

He tried to call the number but there was no reply. It must be Kelly. He switched on the app and saw that Sheryl's symbol was somewhere in Birkenhead. Would they know that he knew where she was? He'd have to risk it. He tried to phone Lathom, but the phone just went to answering machine. He grabbed his coat. He still had Lathom's arsenal in the boot of his Range-Rover; he'd decide what he needed when he got to Birkenhead.

A few minutes later, he pulled up across the road from an industrial unit close to Cammell Laird's shipyard. Melville checked his phone, this was where Sheryl's phone was but whether she was here in person was a different matter. He opened the boot of his car and sorted through Lathom's belongings, looking for inspiration. He assumed that Kelly wouldn't be alone so he needed a gun, but that wouldn't be sufficient to deal with Kelly himself. He looked at the bomb that Lathom had found under his car, this would be perfect but he didn't have an easy way to detonate it and he didn't want to kill Sheryl as well. Instead he picked up the cutlass and weighed it in his hand. It had good balance and would make a formidable weapon at close quarters. Then he sorted through the collection of guns and chose the Glock, smaller and much lighter than his Webley, plus it held seventeen rounds rather than the Webley's six. He tucked the pistol in the waist band of his trousers and slowly walked towards the unit which was in darkness, the cutlass in his right hand.

The front of the unit was dominated by a wide shuttered steel door which was opened by a button on the right. He assumed that once he pressed this a motor would open the door, but whoever was inside would be alerted to his presence, Melville pressed his face to the edge of the door and through the gap thought he could see some light coming from inside. He walked around the outside of the building. There was light coming from a small window at the rear but the window was too small for him to climb through but, it seemed likely that whoever was inside was at the rear of the building. He pulled over a wheelie bin and climbed on it, then pressed his ear against the window. He could hear music coming from inside. In that case, perhaps they wouldn't hear the main door opening; it was certainly worth a chance. He returned to the front of the building, took a deep breath and pressed the button.

'What was that noise?' Eloise switched off the ghetto blaster; grabbed the piece of bloody rag and forced it into Sheryl's mouth then went to the door and opened it slightly, peering into the darkness.

'Prince Charming has come calling after all,' she sniggered and, picking up the orange epi-pen, she went through the door closing it behind her. Sheryl knew she had to act now if she was to save Melville and herself from a painful death. She pulled herself onto her knees and, bending backwards, gradually squeezed her handcuffed hands over her feet. Once her hands were in front of her body she pulled her penknife from her bra and began to saw at the ropes around her ankles.

The steel door slowly began to rise, once it had risen enough to squeeze beneath, Melville stopped the motor and slid under it. The unit was empty except for a large car covered by a tarpaulin, and a body lying in a pool of fresh blood. He knelt and was about to turn the body over when there was a flash of light as a door at the back of the room opened and a young girl came running out. He stood up as she ran towards him.

'It was so horrible Richard– thank goodness you've come to save us.'

Melville put down the cutlass, 'How do you know my name?'

'My sister told me about you—don't you recognise me?'

Melville stared at the girl and then hesitantly said: 'Emma? Is it really you—but how?'

Suddenly the door burst open again and Sheryl ran into the room. Melville was surprised by two things: the fact that she was screaming like a banshee and also by the large red fire axe she held above her head. She ran towards them both. Eloise turned, dropped the orange epi-pen she'd been holding behind her back and made a grab for the cutlass on the floor but Sheryl was too quick for her. The first blow of the axe caught her at the back of her neck, Eloise screamed and fell to her knees; the second blow finished her off.

Sheryl leaned on the axe panting for breath. 'Hiya Lee, what took you so long?'

'What? Do you know who that was?'

'Yeah, *your* Emma. To be honest, Lee, I'm getting fed up with your ex's turning up all the time.'

'Look I know you get jealous but did you have to kill her?'

'You and your big head, Lee. I didn't do it because of that.'

'Why then?'

'She used me lippy without asking.'

'What?'

Sheryl took hold off the girl's feet and began to drag the body back towards the room she'd come from.

'Make yourself useful Lee, you bring her head—then you can find the key for these handcuffs.'

Melville picked up the girl's head by the hair and followed her, muttering to himself.

A short while later they were in shower room while Eloise's body fizzed in the bath next to them; Melville was having difficulty taking it all in. Sheryl had touched up her make-up and was playing with the orange epi-pen.

'So they drugged you with that and brought you here. You sure it was Isabella and not Kelly?'

'Positive. She even introduced herself. I haven't seen any sign of Kelly.'

'Who's the dead man next door?'

'Don't know. He must be some Italian; she said he was called Dino. It seems that these girls don't cope with rejection too well—they wanted to hurt me to get back at you.'

'I need to talk to Isabella. Perhaps it was only Emma who wanted revenge for what I did.'

'You don't get it—she was already dead when you murdered her but you couldn't sense that she was a vampire at the time. They set you up. She wasn't there to bring Isabella's husband his gloves but to kill him if you chickened out.'

'I need to talk to Isabella, get her to explain.'

'Forget about a quiet chat, Lee. You start the car and I'll get me axe; it's the only thing they understand. The sooner we have her fizzing away the better.'

'I couldn't kill her; I'll explain that it's over between us and ask her to leave us alone.'

'I thought you'd say that, Lee. Sorry about this.'

'About what? Oww! What was that?'

Melville fell to the floor and Sheryl stood over him: 'You're too soft, Soft Lad. You have a nice rest while I sort out Cruella De Ville.'

He lay on his back, aware of his surroundings but unable to talk or move a muscle while Sheryl sorted through Eloise's belongings. She picked up the girl's phone and dialled. He could only hear half of the conversation.

'Hiya, is that the Wicked Witch of the North?'

'She can't come to the phone at the moment—she's in the bath.'

'We need to meet. Where?'

'Another place? Give me an hour—come alone and unarmed?'

Sheryl switched off the phone, knelt beside Melville and searched his pockets. She took his car keys and waved them in front of his face, then leaned over and kissed him on his forehead.

'Sweet dreams, Lee. Don't worry; I'll be back soon with another one in need of an early bath.'

§

Kelly took the lift to the 10ᵗʰ floor. He knocked on the apartment door and as it opened he barged through, knocking Peter to the floor.

'What?' Peter picked himself up and moved away from the door towards the kitchen work surface.

'Well, I said I had some bad news for you.' Kelly held up his arms, 'Is this bad enough?'

'What do you want?' Peter had taken refuge behind the breakfast bar and he looked nervously from side to side for a means of escape. Kelly took a note pad and a pen from his pocket.

'First some details for my records; I like them to be as accurate as possible. Full name including middle names, and age?'

'What? Is that all you want?'

'You heard me—I can fill in the rest later.'

'Peter Charles Truscott, twenty-eight.'

Kelly made a note. 'Good—now, where's the girl? I've got her details already. They'll just need updating.'

Peter, looking around for a means of defence, saw the knife-block on the other side of the kitchen but Kelly saw it too and crossed the room to stand in front of it. In desperation, Peter grabbed the small syringe lying on the work surface next to him and waved it at Kelly.

'You leave Tash alone … I know what you are a vampire. Come any closer and I'll kill you.'

'Oh, please.' Kelly shook his head. 'I know you're stupid—but I'm not. What harm do you think a little prick will do to me?' He looked disdainfully at Peter and his tiny syringe. 'Sorry—two little pricks.'

'It's a virus, a retro virus. It switches on your telomeres—you'll die.'

'You little prick—I've survived yellow fever, smallpox and even ebola with only a headache. Do you think that'll kill me?'

'It killed a vampire mouse.'

Kelly laughed: 'Did it have pointy teeth and wings? I think you'll find that was a bat.'

Kelly lunged forward and grabbed Peter's hand containing the syringe with his good hand, and squeezed; Peter screamed and dropped the syringe. Kelly hit him hard in the stomach with his artificial hand and as Peter doubled up pushed him onto the floor and sat on him. Peter's arms were trapped under Kelly's knees and he was unable to move.

'OK—we can do this the painful way, or the very painful way. Where's the girl?'

'Don't know.' Peter tried to shake Kelly off, but one of his hands was broken and Kelly was much too strong for him.

Kelly held him around the throat with his artificial hand and waved the index finger of his good hand in his face reproachfully.

'I warned you. Now I'm going to gouge out your eye. Tell me where she is I'll let you keep the other one.' He slowly moved the finger towards Peter's face, relishing the terror in his victim's eyes. He loved that look. At least the evening wasn't going to be a complete waste of time. Then his phone rang in his pocket.

'Sorry about this,' he sighed, reaching for it, '– be with you in a minute.'

It was the Contessa and he answered it impatiently.

'Hello, Contessa, I'm a bit busy at the moment.'

'Stephen, we have a problem with the girl. Can you come to the hotel immediately?'

'Immediately?'

'Yes.' She hung up without further explanation.

'Women!' Kelly shrugged and put his hands on either side of Peter's head. 'Sorry, I'd love to have stayed and played but I've got to go—been nice knowing you.'

Then he snapped Peter's neck.

Standing over Peter's body, Kelly looked around the apartment for somewhere to dispose of it. The apartment really did seem familiar—had he been here before? Then he recognised the rug next to the body; it must be the same one—some people had no taste. He bent down and turned it over; the label had been cut off with a knife—his knife.

Kelly smiled. Now he knew what to do with the body; exactly the same as last time. He picked up Peter's corpse and tipped it over the balcony. It landed with a thud in the courtyard ten floors below. It was very late and the rest of the block was in darkness and it wouldn't be discovered until the morning. They might even think it was a suicide like last time. He picked up the syringe from the floor, squirted the liquid into the sink, rinsed it through with water and left it on the floor by the open balcony, then quietly let himself out and walked the short distance to the Hilton Hotel.

§

It was half an hour before Melville properly regained consciousness. He felt slightly shaky as he checked his phone. There was no sign of Sheryl's symbol, perhaps she was wise to his location-finder app and had switched her phone off. How would he find her? She could be walking into an ambush. What had she said: that they were going to meet at 'some other place', well that was obvious so why say it? No, she'd said 'another place', and the way she'd said it, perhaps it was the name of a club or a bar—'Another Place'. If that was the case, how would he find it? What did Sheryl always say: 'When in doubt *Google* it.'

Melville opened his phone and entered: 'Another Place Liverpool'.

ANOTHER PLACE: About 6miles (9.5km) north of Liverpool is Crosby beach. Here you'll find the striking public art work 'Another Place' by world famous British artist Anthony Gormley.

The work consists of 100 cast iron life-size figures spread over 2miles (3km) of lovely coastline. They reach approximately

0.6miles (1km) out to sea, being increasingly submerged and revealed as the tide goes in and out. Each figure weighs 0.7 ton (650kg) and is made from casts of the artist's own body. To see them together is an impressive sight...

Melville now knew where and when, but how to get there in time since Sheryl had taken his car? He tried phoning Lathom but there was only an answer-phone message. He pulled the tarpaulin off the car inside the unit, a large black 4X4. The door was unlocked but he couldn't find any keys, neither in the office nor on the man's body next to it. Needs must: it had been a long time since Melville had stolen a car, but within ten minutes he'd forced the steering lock and hot-wired the ignition. He opened the outer door, threw the cutlass on the passenger seat and reversed out.

§

It had taken Lathom less than half an hour to drive to Chester. He pulled into the gravel drive and used the man's keys to open the front door. He held the John's Browning in his hand and slammed the front door.

'Ah, there you are John.' The old man's voice came from the drawing room.

'Yes sir,' replied Lathom. He walked slowly down the corridor, his flat cap pulled down over his eyes.

'Any difficulties?' asked the old man. He was reading with his back to the door and he didn't look up as Lathom approached.

'None—just like old times,' said Lathom.

The old man turned and saw Lathom.

'It appears that I underestimated you Robert,' he said.

'Yes sir—you always did,' replied Lathom then shot him at point-blank range.

He dropped the gun. Ballistics would show that it had killed all three men. Hopefully the fire would make John's body unrecognisable and with only Lathom's watch and document to go on they would assume that John had killed him, then disappeared. Lathom searched the house for anything of use and found foreign currency and a couple of passports in a wall safe using a key taken from the old man's waistcoat pocket. He left the safe open to make it look like a burglary; he knew the Department wouldn't believe it but at least it would give them a palatable story to feed to the press.

One of the passports was John's and Lathom decided to muddy the waters a little bit more. Wearing the dead man's coat and hat he could probably pass for him on CCTV. He would drive to an airport—Gatwick would be ideal—leave the car in the airport car park, make sure he was seen on CCTV, then dump the clothes and take a train to London. That would buy him a few more days while they trawled through the passenger lists looking for a possible lead.

He stepped outside, closed the front door quietly and listened. No one seemed to have been disturbed by the noise of the gunshot. He carefully reversed the Jaguar off the drive and set the SAT-NAV for Gatwick airport, according to its display he would be there in four hours and six minutes. He looked forward to celebrating the first day of his new life with a fried breakfast; he'd miss the old one but Robert George Lathom was now officially dead. He assumed that, if he really was a vampire as he'd been told, this was something he'd have to get used to, for now this fresh life was a novelty and only time would tell if being a vampire was a gift or a curse. He checked John's watch on his wrist and idly wondered what Sheryl and Lee were up at this moment. He smiled to himself; probably tucked up in bed making up for lost time, he thought.

§

Sheryl pulled into the empty car park and parked facing the sea. The sun had begun to rise behind her illuminating the beach with weak sunlight. The tide was out but a heavy mist clung to the foreshore. She scanned the beach but it appeared completely empty; it seemed that it was too early even for joggers or dog walkers. She could see the 'iron men' dotted across the beach, black silhouettes against the grey Irish Sea. As the mist drifted backwards and forward they disappeared and then reappeared again so that it seemed as though they were moving. She was thinking about Melville, switched on her phone and was about to call him to explain when a car pulled up alongside her, a large white 4X4. The Contessa was in the driving seat, she looked at Sheryl and nodded. They walked in silence to the railings and, leaning on them, looked out to sea.

'What of Eloise?' asked the Contessa.

'Let's just say your partnership has been dissolved.'

'Regrettable. It seems that we underestimated you *sister*?'

'No worries, babe.'

'I despised you, but now I see that we have much in common. At first I hated you but now find that I am warming to you. Perhaps soon we will be great friends.'

'That's funny, babe. It's usually the other way around.'

'All we need to decide is what to do about Richard.'

'Richard?'

'I believe you call him Lee.'

'Do whatever you like, keep him or cut out his heart; I don't care.'

'You have no claim?'

'None, I'm so bored by him.' Sheryl tried to sound disinterested. She needed to know her intentions before taking any further risks.

The Contessa touched her arm, 'You are correct, sister. Men are so predictable.' She squeezed Sheryl's arm and smiled. 'Once we have disposed of our little problem, perhaps we can become better acquainted?'

'Who knows, babe. Change is as good as a rest.'

Another car entered the car park but they couldn't see it due to the mist.

'Let us discuss the matter where we cannot be overheard?' said Isabella. She took off her heels and walked down the concrete steps onto the sand; Sheryl did the same and followed her. The beach was deserted and the mist drifted backwards and forward. They walked out towards the black silhouettes.

§

It was Melville who had pulled into the car park. He checked his phone and he could now see Sheryl's phone symbol nearby although it was too misty to be able to see her car or for her to see his. He still didn't understand what had prompted him to follow her. After all, she'd drugged him and left him helpless. Perhaps he should just let her get on with it; she always did what she wanted, rarely asked him what he wanted for himself. What was this all about anyway—revenge? He could understand why she'd want revenge on Kelly but this wasn't Kelly, it was Isabella, someone he'd once loved. Was she really so jealous or was it just the killing she enjoyed?

He'd wanted to sit down and talk it through; he was sure it could all be sorted out without further bloodshed. Above all, he needed to understand what had happened all those years ago: had he killed Emma or was she already a vampire as Sheryl had told him? Only Isabella knew the whole truth. He deserved to know but Sheryl had left him paralysed, taken his car and gone off to see Isabella with a bag of make-up and an axe.

Of course, if Sheryl was right, there was no reason for him to have felt guilty all these years and he should now accept himself for what he was—a vampire. And start enjoying himself rather than risking life or, more importantly, limb on some territorial dispute. Surely the world was big enough for all of them? What they needed was a truce not a war. The mist was clearing and he was worried that the women would soon be able to see him. He started the car and moved it a few hundred yards further down the road towards Liverpool where he left it, but he couldn't lock it because he had no keys. He checked his weapons: the Glock and cutlass. The large handguard on the cutlass meant he could only use it with his right hand so he'd have to keep the Glock in his left. If it did get nasty a sword would be more use against a vampire at short distance than the gun—no one wanted to lose an arm or leg for eternity. He quietly shut the car door and walked in the direction of Sheryl's symbol through the mist.

Within a few minutes he'd reached the Range-Rover. A large white 4X4 was parked next to it which he assumed to be Isabella's. The Range-Rover was unlocked and Sheryl's phone was on top of the dashboard next to her handbag but there was no sign of either her or Isabella. They must be on the beach. He searched the Range-Rover and was relieved to find Lathom's arsenal still in the boot together with the axe. Perhaps he was in time to avoid the bloodshed after all? First he needed some insurance in case things had already gone too far.

§

The two women walked slowly and silently through the mist, out towards the sea. When they reached the first iron man they paused and the Contessa took her shoe and hit it on the head. It made a 'clonk'.

'All men are like this, sister—dull and stupid. Life is like a game of chess. Man is the king, plodding one square at a time—protected by the queen. She is the most powerful piece on the board—all the other pieces fear her.'

'So is Lee—Richard—your king or mine?'

'Does it matter? The game we're playing has no black or white; all the pieces are grey. We fight for control of the board; the other pieces are of no importance.'

They walked further out, towards another iron man.

'Fight?' Sheryl asked. 'I thought you wanted to become better acquainted, not fight.'

The Contessa laughed. 'Acquainted with a little tart like you?' she said. 'Is that not too amusing Stephen?'

'Stephen?' Sheryl looked around her but could see no one.

'Very amusing Contessa.' The iron man turned, bowed theatrically then put on its hat. 'Now ladies—it's time for the punch line.'

Kelly pulled the Ghurkha's Kukri from inside his coat and handed a bejewelled dagger to the Contessa. Sheryl backed away from them, looking behind her. It was a few hundred yards to her car and safety.

'Why are you doing this—just to get Lee?'

The Contessa laughed: 'It will be his turn next.'

'Why then?'

'For amusement, one needs diversions to relieve the boredom.'

'Do you mind if we get on, Contessa?' asked Kelly. 'The tide is coming in.'

The water had begun to lap around his feet. They slowly advanced towards Sheryl, who pulled her penknife from inside her bra and opened the blade.

Kelly laughed, 'I think you'll need a bigger knife than that.'

'It's big enough.'

'For what?'

'To take out your eye and to make sure she can't turn her nose up at anyone ever again.'

Kelly laughed again: 'I will miss you, Tonto. Who'll look after the Lone Ranger once you've gone?'

'Did someone mention my name?'

Melville walked out of the mist. Lathom's cutlass was in his right hand and Sheryl's samurai sword was in his left.

'About time too, Soft Lad,' said Sheryl. 'Pass me the sword.'

'No,' said Melville.

'What? Stop trying to be funny, Lee. It doesn't suit you.' She tried to take the sword. 'Give it here!'

'No.' Melville pointed the tip at her and held her at arm's length.

'Can it get any better?' said Kelly. 'It's like Wyatt Earp and Doc Holliday having a domestic in the middle of the OK Corral.'

'Shut up!' Sheryl snapped.

Kelly smiled. 'Looks like we have another Mexican stand-off.'

'It is an impasse,' said the Contessa. 'I refuse to be involved in anything Mexican.'

'Call it whatever you like,' said Kelly, 'but how do we get out of it?'

'We vote,' said Melville.

'Wouldn't you prefer to spill some blood?' Kelly asked. 'I've always found it more effective than democracy.'

'We vote,' said Melville, '- then we spill blood.'

'Explain Richard?' said the Contessa.

'We need to make a blood pact to stop this war. If we fight today, some of us will die, the rest of us will bear the scars for eternity. And for what—for revenge? Isabella are you willing to lose an eye or an ear? Kelly what about you—haven't you lost enough already?'

'Point taken,' said Kelly, '- but, for a blood pact we need blood and there's no one else around. So where do we get it from?'

'One of us has to die.'

'Who?'

'That's what we vote for,' said Melville.

'OK,' said Kelly, 'I vote you die.'

'I think it should be ladies first. Who do you vote for, Isabella?'

'I vote for the tart.'

'Sheryl?'

'I vote for Kelly,' replied Sheryl.

'Kelly?'

'Let's get this clear. Once we decide we kill them—then we have a blood pact?'

'Yes.'

'So our pact stops us trying to get revenge in the future. We all agree to put aside our differences. Is that right?'

'Yes.'

'No way, Lee!' shouted Sheryl. 'I won't agree to that. He killed my sister and they both tried to kill me.'

'How many have you killed?' Melville snapped at her. 'How many sisters or brothers? How many have we all killed? What difference does one more make?'

'He killed Charlotte too.'

'I know—but she was no different from one of my 'Emmas' or one of your 'hot dates'.'

'I can't believe you're talking like this Lee. What's happened to you?'

'I'm just doing what you said I should. I've stopped feeling guilty and want to enjoy myself. I don't want to risk everything just for revenge.'

'I won't agree, Lee. Whatever you say, they have to pay for what they've done.'

'It's a pity—but I thought you'd say that, Sheryl.'

'You haven't cast your vote, Richard,' said the Contessa.

'I vote for Sheryl,' said Melville.

'What! Stop it, Lee; it's not funny. Give me the sword—now!'

'I'm really sorry, but it's the only way we'll have peace.'

'Can I change my vote and make it unanimous?' Kelly laughed.

Sheryl tried to back away but she was surrounded. Melville stuck the cutlass tip in the sand and advanced towards her with the samurai sword in his right hand. It had the sharper blade and would make a prefect execution weapon.

'I'll make sure it's quick and painless; I owe you that. I won't let them get their hands on you. Kneel down it'll make it easier.'

'Easier, Lee? You make it sounds like having a haircut. What if I don't want to make it easier?'

'Then I'll let them do whatever they want with you. It's the pact that's important, not how we achieve it.'

'I thought you loved me.'

'Perhaps I did—once, but now I'm bored, bored with being told what to wear, bored with being told what to do, and bored with being called Soft Lad all the time—told I haven't got a sense of humour.'

'You know I was only joking, Lee. Don't do this—I don't want to die.'

'Neither did any of your 'hot dates' but that didn't stop you, did it? Why are you any different?'

Sheryl knelt on the sand and began to cry. Melville walked to her side and raise the sword above his head. 'Lean forward so I can get a clean strike.'

She bent forward exposing her neck.

'Wait!' The Contessa shouted, 'I change my vote. I vote for you, Richard.'

Melville paused, 'Why? I thought this is what you wanted. Sheryl dead then we can be together again.'

'I can no longer trust you, Richard. She trusted you and look what has happened to her. She has no argument with me any longer, while you may still want vengeance. You are more of a threat to me than she is,—I now choose you.'

Kelly laughed and lunged forward grabbing the cutlass from the sand. 'I change mine too. Care to make it unanimous, Tonto?'

Sheryl looked up tears streaking her cheeks. 'No, whatever happens I still want *you* dead.'

'I change mine to you, Kelly,' said Melville. 'That makes it two all.'

Kelly smiled and moved towards the Contessa, the cutlass in his hand, 'Looks like we've another Mexi—impasse.'

They looked from one to another sizing each other up. Each one looking for an advantage. Kelly was unable to hold the cutlass with his left hand due to its guard so held it with his artificial right hand. He realised that in a fight he would be no match for Melville and the Samurai sword. He didn't know if Melville knew this or not. Perhaps it was time to make a deal?

'Can you have a blood pact without blood?' Isabella asked.

'No,' replied Melville, '- but we could have a truce.'

'OK—let's have a truce,' said Kelly, relieved to find a way out of a difficult situation, 'You go your way and we'll go ours?' He stuck the cutlass in the sand bowed and offered the Contessa his arm.

The others looked surprised by the sudden change of events. The Contessa considered her options then, with a smile, took Kelly's arm.

'Thank you Stephen. It's so refreshing to finds a true gentleman in such a place—take me somewhere civilised and warm.'

Kelly and the Contessa turned and walked back towards the car park arm in arm.

'If you come back I'll have your eye in me cocktail,' shouted Sheryl after them.

Kelly waved his hat. '*Au revoir* Tonto,' he called. 'Look after the Lone Ranger for me.'

Sheryl and Melville watched them disappear into the mist in silence.

'Well that went quite well,' Melville seemed amused as he picked up the cutlass.

'What?' Sheryl snapped, 'You offer to cut off my head, then let that psycho and your ex waltz off, and you think it went *quite* well?'

'Well—better than I expected.'

'What?'

'We're both alive aren't we? And have we lost any limbs?'

'Well, yes and no, but -'

'That's what I mean—better than I expected.'

Melville stuck the two swords tip first in the sand, held out his arms, and walked towards her. 'Come here—give me a hug.'

Sheryl wiped away a tear, 'You don't get away with it that easily, Lee. You've got a lot of grovelling to do yet. I expect a decent prezzie and that holiday you've been promising me.'

He put his arms around her and squeezed her tight.

'I really thought you were going to do it, Lee,' she sniffed.

'Sorry, I had to make you believe me—then they would too.'

'How did you find me?'

'I heard you talking to Isabella and looked up 'Another Place' up on my phone.'

'But how did you get here?'

'I hot-wired a car.'

'Robbed a car? I'm impressed; we'll make a Scouser of you yet. All we need to do is work on the jokes. That last one wasn't very funny.'

They walked slowly back towards the car park, the swords tucked under Melville's left arm and his right arm around Sheryl's shoulder.

'Don't you think they'll come back, Lee?'

'Perhaps not. None of us wants to end up maimed for eternity. It's in all our best interests to keep out of each other's way.'

'Do you really think Kelly will give up his vendetta or that Isabella will calmly walk away when I've killed her *sister*?'

'We'll worry about that another day. Let's go out tonight to celebrate.'

'Celebrate what?'

'I don't need to feel guilty any longer. You were right all along, guilt is overrated. Why not enjoy ourselves, it's no good crying over spilled blood.'

His Range-Rover stood alone in the car park. Scrawled across the windscreen in red letters were the words: 'SEE YOU AROUND SUCKERS'.

'See, I told you so, Lee—and he's only gone and used me best lippy too.'

They got into the car and Melville put the swords on the back seat.

'OK—Where do you want to go to celebrate?'

'How about that Japanese restaurant in Duke Street? Give them a call, Lee, and see if they can fit us in?'

Melville patted his pocket. 'I wonder where I've left my phone?'

'Not again, Lee—you'd lose your head if it was loose.' Sheryl realised what she'd just said and they both laughed. She took out her phone and opened the case.

'Hang on, I'll do it,' said Melville as he took the phone from her. 'They can never understand your accent.'

He scrolled down the contacts past the restaurant until he reached *Soft Lad,* and pressed call. As it rang there was a loud bang somewhere in the distance and the car shook slightly.

'What was that, Lee?'

'The end of a beautiful friendship.'

Sheryl gave him a puzzled look. 'Was that supposed to be a joke, Lee?'

Melville smiled and closed the phone.

Epilogue

Two weeks later, Lathom was in his new shop. He'd only got the keys the day before and he still had a lot of work to do before he would be ready for business. First he needed to get some stock; he'd sold all his collections before moving to Liverpool. He planned to visit a local auction next week and had already placed several bids on on-line auction sites. Soon he'd have enough items to put a window-display together. He wasn't too worried about making a profit; he had Kelly's money to live off. And he had a new identity: he was now Geoff Davies antique dealer and specialist in militaria. He had a shop in a leafy part of North London and he even had a National Insurance number.

Lathom had decided to change his appearance along with his identity. He'd shaved his head and begun to grow a goatee beard. A visit to Camden Market had provided him with a collection of Hawaiian shirts and a porkpie hat. He'd recently stopped eating as much, so he assumed that his changes were almost complete, but he had yet to *sense* another vampire and until that happened he was still unsure exactly *what* had actually happened to him. All he could be sure of so far was that it was very unlikely that he would be recognised by any of his former colleagues. He was considerably fitter than before, had lost several stones and looked ten years younger.

He checked his watch, a recent purchase. He'd thrown John's in the Thames—it had been the last link to his old life. It was nearly lunchtime and he set out to explore the area around his shop, which was down a cobbled alley that connected Hampstead High Street to Hampstead Heath. He walked towards the heath, a small Victorian pub stood a little way down the alley. Lathom had spent most of his adult life in pubs and he automatically gravitated towards it. He had never been in this one before but as he pushed open the heavy door he immediately felt at home. He took a seat at the bar. Alcohol no longer affected him but it had stopped tasting strange, so he could enjoy camaraderie of fellow drinkers once again.

'Afternoon sir, what can I get you?' the barman asked as he polished a glass.

'Whisky—double.' Lathom peered at the line of bottles behind the man, recognised an unusual one and pointed to it. 'That one, third from the left.'

The barman poured his drink. 'Don't sell many of these—you a connoisseur of Irish whiskies?'

'No an antique dealer—it was the favourite of a friend of mine.'

'Was?'

'He's dead.'

The barman looked embarrassed and went to serve another customer while Lathom sipped his drink and thought of Danny Corcoran. He looked at the line of bottles on the mirrored shelves behind the bar, all different sizes, shapes and colours from all around the world—just like people. His eyes scanned the shelves searching for familiar brands from his past life: the Old Man's single malt was there, next to it Tom Richardson's Jack Daniels. Jean had always loved her G&T's—but it always had to be Gordon's gin. Lathom suddenly felt lonely.

They were all dead.

Then he smiled because he recognised a squat clear bottle next to the Gordon's. It was Sheryl's beloved Liverpool Gin.

He raised his glass and toasted, 'Absent friends.'

§

It was an early summer morning. Melville and Sheryl lay in bed; she had her head on his chest and he was stroking her hair.

'That's a nice way to start the day Lee.'

Melville murmured his agreement and added: 'What shall we do now?'

Sheryl giggled and he felt a roaming hand. He reached under the duvet and moved the hand.

'Spoil sport,' she looked up at him and pulled a face like a petulant child, then she smiled and added: 'Don't mind—any ideas?'

'We could go for a walk.'

'Walk!' She sat bolt upright in bed. 'You're inviting me on one of your walks?'

'Well—you're always curious about where I go.'

'You going to take me to meet your wife and six kids in Toxteth?'

'No—not today.' They both laughed. 'Thought I might take you to meet a friend of mine.'

'It's not another ex is it, Lee? I wasn't keen on the last one.'

'Just a friend, you'll like her.'

'Hope so, and she's bound to like me—everyone does.'

Melville was about to say something but decided not to. He changed the subject.

'How are things with Natasha and the baby?'

'OK, all things considered. She goes for her scan next week then she'll know if it's a boy or girl. She's thinking about names at the moment. I suggested Bobby-Lee after you and her Granddad. I thought it was dead clever; you could spell it Bobbi-Leigh for a girl.'

Melville laughed.

'What's so funny, Lee?' Sheryl asked, 'That's exactly what she did.'

Melville quickly changed the subject yet again.

'Have they had the inquest yet?'

'No, next month—do you really think Pete committed suicide?'

'No—do you?'

She shook her head. 'I'm sure Kelly had something to do with it.'

'Well, we'll never know now.'

Melville slid down the bed, turned on his side and stroked her leg.

'Thought we were going for a walk Lee?'

'Perhaps we could get our exercise another way?'

She giggled and slid down next to him. They embraced and kissed.

'I thought you wanted me to meet your friend today?'

'It'll wait. Like you once said—"We've got all the time in the world".'

THE END

COCKTAIL RECIPES

SHERYL'S LIVER BIRD.

3 measures of 'Liverpool' gin.
1 measure of vermouth.

Stir the ingredients in a mixing glass with ice.
Strain into a Martini glass. Garnish with up to three
Maraschino cherries.

THE CONTESSA'S BELLINI.

2 measures of chilled champagne.
1 measure of white peach puree.
1 teaspoon of sugar syrup.
1 dash of grenadine.

Skin a large white peach, then puree it.
Pour the puree into a chilled champagne flute.
Add the sugar syrup and grenadine, stir gently.
Then slowly top up with the chilled champagne.
Garnish with a slice of fresh peach.

ILLUSTRATIONS

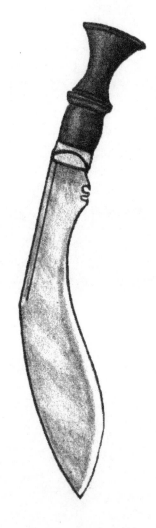

Kelly's Kukri

The Contessa's Arabian Jambiya

Above: Eloise's Ottoman Khanjar

Opposite: 'Another Place'

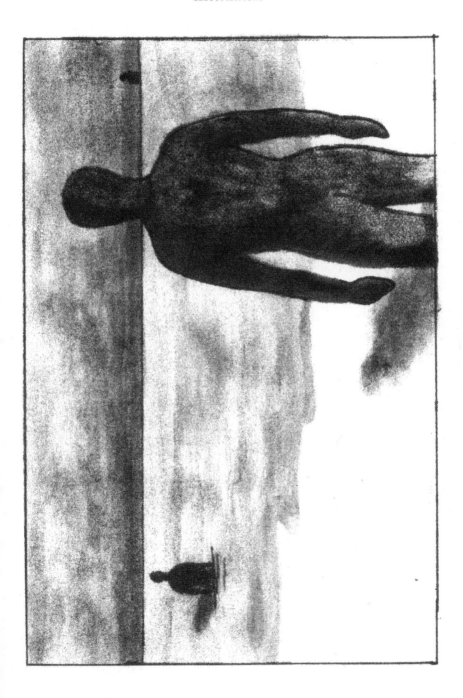